my June

ALSO BY DANIAL NEIL

The Killing Jars (2006)

Flight of the Dragonfly (2009)

The Trees of Calan Gray (2014)

my
June

DANIAL NEIL

RONSDALE PRESS

MY JUNE
Copyright © 2014 Danial Neil

RONSDALE PRESS
3350 West 21st Avenue
Vancouver, B.C. Canada V6S 1G7
www.ronsdalepress.com

Typesetting: Julie Cochrane, in Granjon 11.5 pt on 15
Cover Design: Julie Cochrane
Paper: Ancient Forest Friendly FSC Recycled — 100% post-consumer waste,
    totally chlorine-free and acid-free.

Ronsdale Press wishes to thank the following for their support of its publishing program: the Canada Council for the Arts, the Government of Canada through the Canada Book Fund, the British Columbia Arts Council, and the Province of British Columbia through the British Columbia Book Publishing Tax Credit program.

Library and Archives Canada Cataloguing in Publication

Neil, Danial, 1954,- author
   my June / Danial Neil.

Issued in print and electronic formats.
ISBN 978-1-55380-335-5 (print)
ISBN 978-1-55380-336-2 (ebook) / ISBN 978-1-55380-337-9 (pdf)

   I. Title.

PS8627.E48M9 2014   C813'.6   C2014-901601-8   C2014-901602-6

At Ronsdale Press we are committed to protecting the environment. To this end we are working with Canopy (formerly Markets Initiative) and printers to phase out our use of paper produced from ancient forests. This book is one step towards that goal.

Printed in Canada by Marquis Book Printing, Quebec

for Herb

ACKNOWLEDGEMENTS

I would like to express my gratitude to Ronald Hatch whose certainty of what my story could be helped me mine the greater depths of consistency and meaning.

How does one thank someone who has gone missing? Perhaps nothing is absolutely gone. Rhody Lake was my first Creative Writing instructor in Langley, British Columbia. It was 1987 when I made a conscious decision to be a writer. I remember her clear blue eyes and calming smile. Our class formed a writer's group after the course. It was during those meetings that we read our work aloud to the group. Rhody did not criticize or judge any weaknesses in form or structure. We were just beginning our writing journey after all. No, she encouraged what was good. She focused on our strengths. That has made all the difference. Rhody Lake went missing near her home in Sechelt, British Columbia, in 2005.

I long to reach my home and see
the day of my return.
It is my never-failing wish.

— HOMER, *The Odyssey*

Seaside

JUNE CALLED ME TO say that coffee was ready. A few minutes later, when I came into the kitchen I saw coffee spilled on the floor and our favourite cups broken. I hadn't heard a thing. That she was lying there didn't make sense to me. I knelt down and took her arm, held her limp hand. I felt for a pulse but couldn't find it. I couldn't find her life. I was frantic, shockingly helpless. I heard an inhuman cry, and it was a moment before I realized that it was my own. How could I have been upset about those old cups of ours that we had kept forever? It didn't matter. Nothing mattered. There was only the harsh recognition of something lost and irretrievable. She was gone, and the steam from the pool of coffee lingered, then vanished. As if it were her last breath, and I had wasted even that.

The mind will have its way after the immediate shock of death — the numb and mechanical carrying-on of self-preservation. I remained in a loop of that morning for three months, unwilling, unable to move beyond it. I kept remembering, as if there were something I had missed, that I had failed to do. But one day life will pitch you out like a dog in the rain. You will feel the full force of your loss, the hard loneliness. There will be no avenue that will save you from it, no remedy in a bottle or book. So I did the only thing I could think of, I walked.

I put on my coat and Tilley hat, the one she had picked out for me, to match her own still hanging on a peg in the laundry room, and went downtown. I walked without much vigour, I'm afraid, a sort of aimless stroll along the sidewalk. Then I turned and looked behind me, down Main Street through the thinly falling rain. It was as if someone were calling me. Perhaps it was June or the wind or nothing at all. But I noticed I did that often now, staring like that. And then I remembered the summer and the tourists. They were enchanted with the town and its boldly coloured buildings, a whimsical palette. Some structures had remained for over a hundred years. They loved the streetscape of hanging baskets, banners for all the seasons, benches to rest on, decorative street lights, a charm the world longed for, a safe place, somewhere that seemed immune to the frenetic expansion of cities where growth had become a societal imperative.

It was that very charm that had brought us to Seaside on the Sunshine Coast when our own retirement came striding over the hill. The first brochure arrived like salvation, and we were quick to decide to move. Oh, June was excited. Why wouldn't she be? You can feel it in her letter to the girls after we were settled in the little town:

Dear Lori and Mandy,

Hope all is well at school. No more school for me. Staff gave me a wonderful send off. And your father was speechless when his department gave him a set of golf clubs. (I guess they didn't know he vowed never to golf again after he drove a golf cart into a pond at Shaughnessy and crippled one of the resident swans. Thankfully it survived to duck another ball.) But the reception at city hall was nice. Even the mayor was there. I was so proud of your father. Well, girls, you're going to love this town. There's something for everyone in Seaside. Main Street rules.

There are hairstylists (big demand for those snowy perms — I'll be there soon, I'm sure), a hardware store for the handy (hope for your dad, ha, ha), gift shops and art galleries to die for and a post office with its essential flags and brick. Can you believe it, Barnacle Bob's Fish and Chips? Then there's the Sand Dollar Café, Salty Dog Used Books (your dad's favourite store), dollar store for the miserly and five churches (for those who think God is on their team — sorry about that, it's just me), a grocery store (because we have to eat after all, and you'll love the organic produce).

Seaside has all the small town comforts for the many retirees. And there are a lot. All those lodges and orders. The marina is just below Main Street. There are seagulls dropping clams from rooftops and always the salted air. It seems to remind you of your place in the world. And those street names: Clipper and Yacht and Frigate and Ketch. We'll live on Dory Avenue, adorable, don't you think? Well, lots of hugs from us both. We'll call when we get settled.

Love,
Mom and Dad

She had written that letter in the summer. Now in the fall, clouds rolled in off the Salish Sea. Life had slowed, street trees turned a sunny yellow, an illumined moment in the dull and grey hiatus. I continued on with my walk down the street and across an intersection. The rain picked up. I could hear it thrumming on the parked cars. It bounced from the pavement, leaping bullets, a flood from the rent and brooding bellies of clouds. I drew up the collar on my raincoat and looked down the hill to the marina. I wanted to go there, to look at the name painted aft and stern, touch it with my hands — to see her face with my fingertips. But such images were cruel just then, a savage remembering.

I stopped in the middle of the street and lifted my face and raised my hands like a survivor from some horrible wreckage. It seemed the rain wanted something from me, perhaps to punish me, castigate me for my many imperfections. It dared and taunted and tempted. It fell in translucent sheets over me. It ran down my neck, and I wanted to die, to be

washed away. I could not think of a way out, only the depths of emptiness everywhere, her absence, all meaning cored out of me, hollow and
destroyed.

And in the street with drivers slowing to look at an old fool, they
might have seen the glaze of death in my eyes that I willed in the re-
morseless and urgent rain. But I couldn't stay there forever and wait for
the end of my miserable affliction, my life. I lowered my head and turned
to the looks of strangers as they passed, aghast they seemed, to have come
upon something mad in their midst. Then I turned and crossed the
street. I would go there, damn it all, to Seaside Marina. Under the cover
of an awning I removed a handkerchief from my pocket and wiped the
tears from my face. I removed my hat and dried my neck. I felt old just
then. I knew my face would be pink, with my blood pressure showing
through my thin white hair.

I came up to a shop with pottery in the window. A sign read: "Lessons." I stopped to have a look and stood there dazed, uncertain of everything. There was a bowl and vase — a deep Mediterranean blue. That
colour distracted me now, the colour she had loved; the flowerpots on
the front steps and the canopy and mainsail cover brilliant under a noon
sun. Then I stepped up to the window and cupped my eyes to peer inside. There was a group gathered around a woman at a potter's wheel,
red muck slick on her hands, shaping a spinning lump of clay. They all
seemed to be enjoying themselves. I had to turn away because joy was
impossible. I felt heartsick to see it now, to see it in others, as if life had
abandoned me, removed me, exiled from the shores of paradise that we
landed on such a short time ago. She was the potter and the captain and
the setting sun. And I was something in her hands.

Nelson

MARINER STREET ENDED at the marina. It was shrouded in a drift of rain and fog. My face was soon wet with it, my hard mouth salted. The ocean seemed to melt away at the end of the dock — the last boats with their masts and rigging fading, disappearing. And attached to the shore and set on piers over the rocks and tides, the marina office and store. It was a shoebox of minimalist design, whitewashed and festooned with starfish and shells and all manner of ropes and nets and floats as if it were some hazardous rock that caught those straying or floundering.

I looked down the dock to find her in her berth, but all was lost in a tangle of dim and fuzzy things. A heron was hunched on a boat, the hump of it motionless, imperturbable. And above the fog, the unseen gulls cried for the world to reappear. It was only the miscreant crows scavenging about the rocks and pools that thought it agreeable to their moods and ways.

It did not invite me now, to go down among the boats in such gloom. I turned to the neon sign over the door, "Marine Supplies," a beacon against the cold creep of the sea. I thought I might go in, to have a look, get out of the chill. How I had avoided this day, to see our boat idle, awaiting June's return. I didn't mind Nelson, the owner, but I hadn't been down to the marina since we last took her out against the stiff westerly that jumped us out in the strait. *She did well*, she had called out to Nelson as he took the bow line and snugged us in. Nelson knew his boats, admired the lines of her, the blue trim of a spirited Contessa 32.

I opened the door and he was standing behind the counter. God, when I first saw him I was certain Gordon Pinsent had left the east coast for a taste of Pacific salt and cod. June agreed and teased me to ask him. *Go on, it's Gordon Pinsent. Ask him.* And then Nelson Grommet opened his mouth, and nothing of rankling fits or lore from St. John's — no maritime devil in his eyes, not an east coast boy or a Boston boy, but something in the middle. He was a southern man from the remote and distant Mississippi, who had left by his own account for the sea and sanity. Well, I was not so sure of the latter, but still he was the only man who could help me now.

"Now, Mr. Dale," he said, "it's not a day for sailors."

"Reuben," I told him.

"Reuben then," he said. "You can never be sure of what to call a man right off. I saw you the one time with your wife. Sorry about your troubles. I wouldn't want to be so bold to think we're on a first name basis."

I took that for his condolences. "Thank you," I said. "I began it all, calling you Nelson."

"That's my name. Nelson Grommet. It comes from the old French, you know. Somewhere it has been lost. And look, a bag of them behind me here — all brass. Funny world, isn't it?"

"Amazing," I said. I was struggling with such mysteries.

"I'll bet you have the same thing with your Reuben sandwich." His eyes flared, astounded.

"Yes," I said agreeably. I watched him. Nelson liked to talk. There hadn't been many boaters down to the marina with the weather holding fast against the coast. I suppose he had to let it all out. And I would have liked to carry on with the conversation, but really, to sit down to a Reuben sandwich was lunch and not the aligning of the stars.

I noticed a table in the corner with two chairs and a blue tablecloth. I was drawn to it and the windows with a view up the beach and out to sea. Not much to see beyond the grey drizzle of rain but a quaint spot with ceramic fish swimming on the sills and an electric fireplace that gave a sense of warmth. There was a blue porcelain coffee pot sitting on top of it with its imaginary readiness.

Nelson was watching me now. "It was my wife Sally who came up with it," he said. "She wants to put more tables along the window. Maybe make muffins and scones. She's upstairs with her bulletins. She gives weather reports for the boats. She said that sometimes people like a cup of coffee when they come in. That pot there is just a decoration. I have a real pot on now in the back if you care to sit. I charge only a dollar. Real cream and that new-fangled brown sugar. Sit down, Reuben, and I'll bring you out a cup. I promise I won't bother you much."

I removed my coat and hung it on the back of the chair and set my hat on an empty chair. I sat down at the table. The room was filled with marine supplies and fishing tackle. Maps and charts. Photographs of great fish hoisted by giddy fishermen plastered a wall. Another showed the fine boats that had visited Seaside over the years, a few autographed by the long departed rich and famous. There was a photograph of John Wayne and Nelson posing on the dock. Nelson had once been a young man after all. Then I turned to look out over the marina, the unchanging grey, the world stuffed in a jar with cotton wadding. Rain streaked on the windows. I was listless to be sure. I kept wondering what had happened to my life, why I was there at all. It was hard to accept that the life I had before, my career at city hall and June with her school and students, was gone. If only I could find it. Reality is a shocking thing. It feels like a sharp pain in the ribs, an ache, something disrupted in the unfeeling brain, a blow to the chest and the slow suffocation that seems will never end. I had to see the doctor. I needed help.

"There you go," Nelson said. He set my coffee down, a big white mug with orcas leaping up the sides.

"Thanks," I said. He stood looking out the window, not in a way that one considers the day or the weather, but intent in his looking, something there that subdued him.

"That's a strange thing," he said, "Someone down on the dock. Same as yesterday and the day before. Stands there for an hour then leaves."

I turned to see for myself. I could see something, a shape, dark and motionless. It could have been anything. "You've got good eyes, Nelson."

"Well, a sailor needs good eyes," he said quite soberly. "I was a mate on the tugs and barges taking the limestone from Texada Island down the strait and up the Fraser River to the cement plants. I can see through fog well enough. And I'm uneasy about that business there. I'll just put on my slicker and pay him a visit."

I sat with my coffee as Nelson pulled a raincoat off a hook near the door and slipped out. I watched him as he moved along the dock. He leaned into his steps. Nelson seemed to have a purpose, a place in the world, a reason that made sense to him, things to understand. Something didn't seem right to him. There were two shapes now, and then one of them suddenly hurried back up the dock toward Main Street. The other remained, Nelson I knew, staying there for a few minutes to have a look around. Then he came up the dock with that same pitch over his feet, the same purpose. I waited, curious. He came in through the door and hung up his coat, the rain dripping from his woolly head.

"Some young fella'," he said walking over to me, "just standing there looking at a boat. He wore one of those jackets the kids wear, with those hoods. Never showed his face. I startled him and he left."

"It could be he was just admiring it." I saw no reason for Nelson's suspicion, but I suppose he had a good reason to be vigilant with all that property floating under his care.

"That might be so," Nelson said, "but it was your boat he was admiring."

I finished my coffee. I stood up and put on my coat and hat. I left a dollar on the table. Nelson stood at the window, bothered now it seemed by the things he didn't understand. I thanked him and left. Out in the rain I felt cold all at once. It was quick against my skin — its damp discomfort. Looking down the dock, I wondered who that had been among the boats, what he wanted with her.

Contessa 32

ANOTHER DAY OF RAIN but it was supposed to clear in the afternoon. I stood outside the Seaside Medical Clinic. I didn't want to go in as I didn't know the doctor that well. I wondered what I would say. I looked at my hands; they were shaking and my heart was beating too fast. Then the door opened and a woman left the clinic, holding the door open for me. I checked in at the reception desk then sat down. The room was crowded. No one talked. Most of them were my age. I looked down at the rainwater dripping on the floor. Dark stains on the carpet. I thought I should remove my hat. It would be poor manners if I didn't. And I hadn't thanked the woman who held the door open for me. Things weren't going well. I closed my eyes and waited for my name to be called.

One by one, and an hour later, "Reuben Dale," a nurse finally called out. I followed her down the hall and into a tiny examination room. She smiled then closed the door behind her. Again I sat, all alone now in a bright sterility, an unnerving silence. I could hear my body, the tense rushing of my blood, my heart beating in my ears like a driving engine, a marathon in all that stillness — my muted ruination. Then a rustle outside the door. The door opened and the doctor entered the room. He closed the door, sat on a chair opposite me, and proceeded to look at a blank chart. Then he set it aside.

"Mr. Dale, have we met before?" the doctor asked. He sat forward with his elbows resting on his knees. His stiff white smock like a partition.

"You saw my wife at the hospital, Dr. Chu," I said. Then my voice failed me, a breathless croak. "She was brought into Emergency. In the summer." I remembered my hat and removed it and palmed my hair.

"Yes, of course," Dr. Chu said. "She had a stroke. I'm so sorry."

I nodded, looking down at my hat turning in my hands. It sounded so blunt. When I looked up, I could see that he cared. He had kind brown eyes and seemed to be a patient man.

"So, how can I help you today?"

"Well, I don't know," I said. I felt uneasy talking about myself and a bit foolish for my answer. In all my life I had never had a reason to see a doctor other than for a sprain or a fever. You could account for such things. But now I had nothing to point to.

"Grieving is different for everyone," Dr. Chu said. "It is a most difficult but necessary journey. Can you tell me more about how you feel?"

"I kind of want to give up, I guess. I don't feel like doing anything. I just walk."

"It is good that you walk," the doctor said.

"Mainly because I don't want to be in the house," I said. I couldn't name the unnameable: the utter silence and loneliness like something gnawing on my bones. It had a voice and it screamed with a soundless fury.

Dr. Chu stood up from his chair. "Well then, Mr. Dale, remove your coat and shirt and sit up on the table. I'll have a look at you."

I sat on the table, naked from the waist up, my body blushing in the uncomfortable cold. My belly hung over my belt. I felt self-conscious and tried to hold it in. Dr. Chu placed a cuff on my arm and inflated it.

Then he deflated it, listened to my heart and lungs and then peered into my eyes and ears. He was quiet in his work. Then he stepped back and cocked his head thoughtfully.

"Your blood pressure is elevated, Mr. Dale," he said. "This is a concern." Then his mouth turned grim all at once. "Tell me more about giving up."

I wagged my head side to side, searching for the right words. How to tell someone about something that arrived like a dismal wind, so strange and ruthless, the dissolution of one's very self. "I'm having a hard time," I said finally. It might have been vague but it was the truth at least.

"Depression?"

"Yes. My nerves are bad."

"Western medicine treats the symptoms when we're not well," Dr. Chu said. "There are medications that might give you relief. But there are other things you might find helpful. In the front office you will find brochures. Grief groups and counselling. Volunteering could be beneficial. Think about it. But keep walking. Mindful walking. It is very good therapy for everyone. I will give you a prescription for a sedative. It is a mild tranquilizer that you can take when you need it. Then come back and see me in a month. We'll see how you are then."

I dressed as Dr. Chu wrote out the prescription. "Thank you, doctor," I said. I didn't know for what exactly. I was so confused about life. But it seemed to me that just talking about it helped somewhat. And I knew Dr. Chu had seen it all before.

"You told me about your daughters that day," Dr. Chu said, standing with the door open.

"Yes," I said. "They had to come all the way from Toronto. They were so unprepared . . ." I couldn't say anything more just then. The devastation in their eyes. How they held on to me.

"Talk to them about this. Yes, talk to them. And a good friend to talk to is always beneficial." He handed me a small square of paper. Some doctor-scribble.

I nodded, so agreeable. *She* was my best friend. It had always been enough. I had believed that my life would just go on and on that way forever — the both of us as constant as the tides, sailing up the strait under a fair-weather sky or down, walking along the promenade that followed the Seaside shoreline, wearing our matching hats and coats, a tandem, a team, inseparable. We would be holding hands and no one would ever know it was June who held *my* hand. She was the one plotting the course and trimming the sails. These things I could not say to Dr. Chu, nor could I point to the colour of my eyes and tell him they once were the deepest blue. It was always her of course, living there with her dreams.

"I will arrange for blood work," he said as I left his office. "They will be expecting you at the hospital."

Great. "Thanks," I said.

I had my prescription filled at the drugstore. There was more waiting with the hushed and anxious. They were the ones standing at the ends of the aisles with their worries buried behind thin smiles, patient men in golf jackets and women in polar-fleece vests patterned with wolves and loons. I was the newly incarnated, grim and graceless, awaiting my allotment of pills. And then to the hospital and the rubber knot cinched uncomfortably on my upper arm and the rush of my blood into glass vials. Such routine for the bored technician. I suppose she had seen it so many times before — the beginning of the end. *What terrible things lurk in this old man's blood?* Then back out in the street. It was always a choice now, where to go, what to do. Once it had seemed the ultimate freedom. It had been a goal, a destination that I longed for. But retirement came with no instructions, no rules to follow. Things did not just manifest out of nothing to entertain me and fill my days. I never had a plan.

June had a plan. She would tutor English and math in the fall. Retirement was not an ending for her but a beginning. Oh, I had heard it all, the pitfalls and snares for the unprepared. I was never worried about keeping busy. I was satisfied in just watching her, listening to her plans, how we would sail up the coast to Alaska and then circumnavigate Vancouver Island in readiness for California and beyond. Nothing daunted her.

So what could I do now with the clouds parting and the sky bleeding through? I could go back to the house we bought on Dory Avenue, that we fell in love with, its cedar beams and river-stone exterior, that fine wrought-iron fence and gate — a west coast house for sure, and those summer garden beds with scarlet geraniums and royal blue petunias, sword fern in the shadows, and her with a little shovel and dirty knees and that smile that proved without a doubt that dreams do come true. I could not go there so easily. She was there, everywhere, in the paintings, the furniture, the collection of pottery — and the colours that broadcast such promise, such good and hope. How careful she was in her selections with her fine tastes, her temperament for details, *the aesthetic*, she would say. I would sit sometimes and wonder how she did it all. It was not so easy to live there now, to finger the things she had touched and loved. So I walked, a walking fool. Like Forrest Gump before he started to run. *Walk, Reuben, walk.* The mantra of survival, of preservation.

On my way to the marina the sun bore through the agents of autumn, the sticky clouds that clung to the forested mountains above Seaside. They had to yield, finally, lest I fall in a heap and die awash in the gushing streets. So much melodrama, but I was soothed when the boats came blinding back into the world. Down on the dock, there was life now, sailors, and townsfolk out for walks, milling, reacquainting with their fellows. The sun mooned in the placid water of the marina and dazzled out in the ripples beyond the breakwater. And I could feel something in me now, an eagerness to get it done: to go back to her. I'll admit that the tiny pill took the edges off my dread. There was shame too, that I needed such a thing. But still it was a relief and I was grateful just then.

There was a couple, my age perhaps or older, sitting aboard their sloop with glasses of wine. I knew how that was. Just to be aboard, tied to the cleats, safe, and the sea always in the background as if our lives were pinned to it. We did that — just as they did now. It nearly took me to my knees. I wanted to jump aboard and hold them, tell them to savour every drop of their lives. You may never drink from that glass again. But why would I disrupt such a moment? Then I could see her, as I neared the berth, the gleam of her wetted hull, never taking my eyes away until I could see the first glimpse of her, seductive in that cursive blue, *my June*, like a friend and lover.

I stood there expectant but fearful, waiting for a feeling, perhaps restoration, something reassuring, something that felt like a touch or a whisper. But there was only emptiness and the lap of water and the rub of fenders. The life I had given the boat was all at once fugitive and inert, a thing dead against the laugh and quarrel of gulls. What things had my mind contrived? And then Nelson's voice from the fuel dock, and I looked over to him across the marina. He was calling to me, pointing. I turned and that kid was just standing watching me, not ten steps away, with his eyes only shadows under his hood, just as Nelson had said the day before.

"What do you want?" I asked him right out.

He had turned first to Nelson's voice, seemingly undeterred, then back to me. He raised his head and his vague eyes told me nothing. His hood that invoked suspicion in me, a contemptible guise.

"Is that your boat?" he asked. A young voice.

"Yes, why do you keep coming down here to look at it?" There was such unease in me now, a deviation from the normal things of sea smells and boats and the gold and russets of hardwoods above the shoreline.

"You named it after her," he said.

My stomach clawed all at once, and I felt a great temper rush swift to my hands. I stepped toward him, but he must have seen the rage in my eyes and backed away. "What do you want?" I growled now, and the people on the dock stopped and stared. I felt violated and didn't know why.

Then he turned and ran. I called out to him to stop, but he only looked over his shoulder as if measuring my resolve. I couldn't let him get away. Although I was in no physical condition to chase him down, I had to find out what he wanted. I ran after him in my awkward way. Nothing fluid in my limbs, as if I had forgotten the basic things from some other time. And in front of me: the blur of pumping legs, a boy in flight.

Nelson came up from the fuel dock, and intercepted me before I reached the hill. The kid had stopped running. It seemed he was a fair judge of my abilities. But still he kept looking back. Then he walked backwards for a ways to make sure. A smudge in the bright afternoon.

"Reuben," Nelson said, "you don't know what you're dealing with there. It's not like the old days. Some of the young ones don't have a care to stick a knife in a man."

The kid was walking easy now as if he thought that I'd quit on him.

I was breathing hard. "I'll just see where he goes," I said starting up the hill.

"Be careful," Nelson called out.

I turned. Nelson Grommet was another man in the world. The sun was on his back. "Look at this," he added. "It's why they call it the Sunshine Coast."

Jonas

✑

IT WAS A LONG CLIMB for me, and I lost him at the top of the hill. I was a walker now, it was true, but hauling my stumpy legs up that grade without rest or pause bent me double. My lungs burned and I held my knees. How would I have grabbed hold of him, shook the truth out of him? Somehow I had grown old and feeble — the bleakest of revelations, the folly of a man to think that he could assail the unknown. The kid was nowhere to be seen.

I caught my breath. I stood where Mariner Street ended, with the sea below me a sheet of gold in the late afternoon, a trickle of sweat down my hot back. The rousing colours in the yards now and wood smoke rising from the chimneys like memories. How a smell can take you back in an instant, unbidden, teleporting you to another time. It would arrive so fresh and new and always known, a string of images, connecting, a sensory profusion. It would always come when the first fires of autumn found me. Suddenly I was a boy back in Ladner where the Fraser River slowed over the marshes and every pickup truck in town had a shotgun mounted in a gun rack with a black lab loose in the back and homes with strings of ducks hanging by their necks in the carport. It was those river places where the fog found the wood smoke and the air so thick and yellow that you couldn't drive in it. All that from a smell.

And then it occurred to me, what a memory was. My life with June was just memories now, moments that were receding. It was if I were somewhere out at sea, and she the wake that drifted farther away, never again to realize how the present leaves the past. I would have to recall her to find her.

The Seaview cemetery wasn't far, where the town ended and the forest began. Sometimes I needed proof that she was gone. Potted mums dotted the lawns, yellow mostly. They always had them down at the grocery store on Main Street. She loved the purple ones, a deep burgundy. She said they reminded her of something enduring. Perhaps the colour of the soul. There was a pot there now, the one I placed a few days before. I could see it down the rows of bronze and granite memorials, her place. The grass was wet and a breeze rising in the maples that bordered the curving inner road. I glanced down at the names as I passed the recent graves, old names like James and Stanley and George and . . . It always startled me.

JUNE DALE

1951–2013

LAY ME DOWN BY THE SEA

I turned away because I couldn't bear to look at it for long and imagine her beneath my feet, wasting away in such darkness until there were only her bones cradled in her pretty blue dress. The mind is a dreadful friend. I couldn't talk to her there as some do with their departed loved ones. I couldn't tell her that we played Crosby, Stills & Nash's "Southern Cross" at her funeral. It was her favourite song. She used to play it in the car when we were driving down to the boat. And how she would sing it with the wind in her hair when I knew she was the happiest in her life.

I looked around me. It was all so beautiful, the lanes of the sun-like fingers reaching from the horizon to find her, and always an eagle with its fine white head illuminated against the forested slopes. But it did not feel like home. Sometimes I just wanted to go back to Vancouver, to Kerrisdale, to our old neighbourhood and all things familiar, to something fluid, the living energy of a city where a family once lived. Now that was a memory, too. Oh, there is always too much past, and the desperation to find it, as if all answers lived there. It seems such a human thing, this searching. Now there was only stillness. *Not a bad spot in eternity with a view like that*, she told me one day after we arrived. It was a joke. How could I abandon her?

Then I heard something from behind me. I had a vigilance now, a wariness with that kid around. It was not the rattle of limbs or the wind soughing through the distant firs, but something that did not belong. The maples were planted some time ago and were evenly spaced and similar in size, their great crowns reaching out across the road. The leaves had fallen in perfect rusty circles around each one. You could not mistake the squeeze of footfall on leaves.

He was behind the tree closest to me. I caught the dark outline of him, a flash of movement like a shutter, visible, and then vanishing as one might spy on the unaware. And he was doing just that. But I was aware, and it seemed that he was not on to my discovery. I would play the game. Damn him — my anger's swift return. I turned back to the grave and knelt down and moved the pot of flowers. A ceremony for him, that kid skulking around the things that I loved. I stood up and said my goodbyes to June and then walked away with my hands clasped behind my back, my head down and a singular gaze at my feet. I moved slowly toward the cemetery road, reflective and angling away from him. And when I met the road I stopped and looked back out across the strait. The sun was setting behind Vancouver Island now, with a grey light falling across the lawns. Just a man alone with his thoughts. I turned, coming back to him now, on my way home, my business in the cemetery finished.

The tree was close, a few steps away over the scattered leaves. I did not look toward it, but he was there and a tightness in my body now as I considered him. I came up alongside it and casually turned, fearful and apprehensive to see his smoking breath hanging as the air began to chill. My steps by degrees, still moving, some stealth emerging that shocked me. I thought myself perhaps misguided, irrational for such a plan. But this I had to do. I was so keen to movement and sound and the stalling of time that the world turned mute and unreachable, with the tension as thick as matter. I waited, measuring.

And then all at once I made my move and vaulted for the tree and reached around it and took hold of his arm. He shrieked and reared back and stumbled. I lost my grip. But still I stood over him with my unacquainted anger. There in the leaves and always that hoodie, hiding like a covert monk.

"What the hell are you up to?" I shouted at him.

"What's wrong with you, old man?"

"You've been down to my boat. Now you're creeping around here. What do you want?"

"I don't want anything."

"That's not good enough!"

"I don't need to tell you anything."

"Just tell me what you're doing here."

"None of your business, you paranoid old fuck!"

"Listen, you little bastard, you said something to me down at the marina. You said that I named it after her. You better tell me what you meant by that!"

"What will you do?"

"Don't tempt me."

"You're going to pop one, old man. You don't scare me." The way he looked at me, something that he detested.

I stood back, shaking, glaring at him. Then my legs felt soft all at once. I didn't feel well. Seeing that, he got to his feet and brushed the leaves from his pullover. He pulled his hood back. I could see him now. He loomed over me, remarkably a sweet-faced boy with dark eyes and hair. Those long eyelashes that girls fall for. But a kid that could kick the ass of some old fool. I leaned against the trunk of the tree to steady myself. How he pinned me there.

"What's wrong with you?" he asked.

"What's your name?"

"Why?"

"Come on."

"Jonas."

"Jonas, you see, I just lost my wife. That was our boat." He only looked at me. Why would he care?

He lowered his head and shrugged. Indifference, but perhaps something else.

"It doesn't matter," I said. "Just stay away from her."

"Her?"

"The boat."

I felt useless. I couldn't sustain my anger. As if it were some new tool to manoeuvre outcomes. *Reuben, he never gets mad*, June used to say. But I didn't care now. I needed to go back to the house, have a shower and make some dinner. It was cold and growing dark. I was all used up. I left him standing there and started walking out to the street. I half-turned and he was coming up behind me. It was strange but I didn't care. He could have clubbed me over the head and robbed me. But he just followed me — a shadow, some intention but undeclared. Then he must have broken away, for when I looked over my shoulder he was gone. The strange meetings that I didn't understand. And then the street lights came on and the sea undetectable now, like iron under the blue-black sky.

The house was dark. I flicked on the outside lights, then the light in the kitchen and lamps in the front room. I turned on the gas fireplace. All the things to give a house its life. I sat down on my recliner, in the silence of aloneness watching the flames flickering yellow and blue. Then I touched the book I was reading, *Anil's Ghost*. Nothing lasts. I could feel the currents of fear returning. The kid, was he watching me now? I could feel him near. What did he want? I reached in my pocket and removed a tranquilizer from the pill bottle. Placing it under my tongue, I sat in the warm light until my eyes found the photograph above the mantle, our family portrait, with Lori and Mandy, teens hiding their braces with closed smiles. They had their mother's blond hair and sympathetic brown eyes. We all wore denim. They went along with it, did it for their dad, some idea that I had, a photograph of the family sitting on a beached log in English Bay and the setting sun like blush on our cheeks. It seemed an accomplishment to me. Something of pride and contentment.

But I should have known the fragile and temporary nature of life. I should have known that nothing lasts. I forgot *him*. I wondered if it was all predestined: the moments counting down, our breaths ticking away until they were all used up. And we would never know the moment of the last one. We were given only so many. It all began with *his* last breath, and the first breath we shared, that December morning in 1971.

Cambie and Twelfth

✒

I DON'T THINK ANYONE thought I would amount to much. My parents did not have great ambitions for the Dale brothers, nothing beyond Grade 10 for Walter and Lyle, and for me, well they knew I was different, a reader of books and never to be found under some wreck in the driveway. But that did not translate into some aptitude that they could recognize. My father was a mechanic, Archie Dale. He had a garage on Elliot Street in Ladner. He was always reeking of oil. His fingers were as thick as pickles with those persistent black fingernails that my brothers inherited when they gladly took up the business of clutches and transmissions. And when I graduated from Delta Secondary School my mother telephoned all her sisters. *Wonderful news, Helen*, they would have said, at that small measure of my success. But it was no small thing to her. She told everyone in Ladner it had seemed, that *Reuben graduated under the academic program*, as if a mechanic's sons were bound to a certain life, a fate of mashed knuckles and grease. And those coveralls my mother could never get clean. They hung on the clothesline like filthy skins.

I never had the hands for real work. They weren't tempted to muck it up, to immerse in anything messy that I had to wipe off. And when college appeared like a possibility, I was pleased to know that a young guy could make a living with his head and not his might and muscle. Business Administration and a Sprott-Shaw diploma. My mother treated me like a doctor. She was so proud. Walter and Lyle too, I remember, bragging me up to their friends. But my father, he was silent about it. Not indifferent. He cared. Oh, I knew he was proud in his own way, but I always worried that somehow I made him feel inadequate. He never was a failure to me. And when it came time to take Walter and Lyle out in the punt when the northern mallards came in, he would look at me as if he knew that something else was waiting for me. But how could he have known? He had a simple, unassuming way. Perhaps he had an unconscious understanding that existed outside the laws of the world. I couldn't explain it. He was the first to know.

Soon after my diploma, I landed my first real job. There was such excitement at home, my mother on the telephone once again: *Reuben's going to be a clerk at Vancouver City Hall. What's a clerk?* She didn't know. I didn't know too much myself, but I was more than eager, anxious too, when I left Ladner that late autumn Monday morning as wet snow began to fall. My first day. I got to drive my father's '65 Chevy Fleetside pickup. My mother waved from the front steps as I headed up the street to join the traffic on Highway 99 that would take me into Vancouver.

I felt important to be sure, on my way to work in the big leagues. My hair was cut short, respectable, just over the ears and I was wearing my father's suit. It was western cut, but it had to do. Since I couldn't afford my own, new clothes would have to wait. I would get my own car after a paycheque or two, perhaps a Mustang or Camaro, and an apartment. My leaping ahead. There was much to think about with the windshield wipers thick with slush as I drove along the freeway. Then I crossed over the north arm of the Fraser River and the traffic slowed on Oak Street. I rolled the window down at a traffic light and reached for the wiper blade and stripped away the gathering ice. I began to worry about being late. It was snowing hard but still wet and not sticking to the road. As the traffic crawled, I kept looking at my watch. It was dark in the city and the snow fell in the headlights like comets.

The trees lining the street were covered in snow now, a magical scene if I hadn't been so preoccupied with the time. I turned off Oak Street at 41st Avenue. I would try Cambie Street. But there was no change, and the snow continued falling in a mute barrage, layer after layer, flakes like shattered clouds. There were children in the crosswalks now on their way to school. I was going to be late, late on my first day. I dreaded the inching down Cambie Street toward 12th Avenue, and Vancouver City Hall on the corner. Then the snow began to stick to the road, and the wipers could not keep up. I wondered about the cars around me, the people going to work. Perhaps they all had the same worries, the same impatience. But a first day and that first impression. I could see the headlines: REUBEN DALE: LATE FOR HIS FIRST DAY AT CITY HALL.

And then I was encouraged, for the traffic began to move as I neared the intersection. But the green light was lost and then the amber too. I wasn't going to make it through. Yet something pushed me on, and I pushed on the accelerator. I had to make it. I told myself that I had time if I could just make the light, reach the other side. I thought I had cleared the intersection, but a shadow appeared in front of me, someone moving from my left — an impression of a person running — then a moment when he turned and I saw his face through the smeared glass, frozen, eternal in silence, the snowflakes falling in his eyes. My foot reached for the brake pedal but it was not enough. There was only an impulse to react. Then the sound of him against the front of the truck, a fleeting recognition of impact, an arm flailing for but a second, then the realization and the truck skidding, the back coming around. The traffic lights, red and green, and buildings rising above me with Christmas lights in the great trees at city hall, all the pretty colours and the world spinning, sliding away and the snow falling, falling. Then all was still, the engine stalled, and I sat unmoving. I didn't know how long. I remember saying to myself, *Oh, my God, I hit someone.*

I heaved myself out of the truck, so afraid of what I might find. Others had stopped to gather around and were looking under the truck. I heard them. He was pinned there in the cold and wet, with blood in the snow. He wasn't moving; there were no sounds. I couldn't reach him. And then sirens and a fire truck. Soon the police and ambulance arrived, and men who could help took over and moved me away, behind the sidewalk where I stood and watched, listening to their urgent voices. One policeman asked me if I was the driver and I told him I was. And there on the back of the curb was an open case and a saxophone bent in the snow.

The world seemed to end. I wanted so much to undo it all, to go back a few minutes, an hour, so that I might have done something different. The job at city hall seemed so unimportant just then. I prayed that he was all right. And I knelt down in the snow and shook. My suit was wet with snow and I was alone, cut out from the world, removed from what I thought was good. How could I go on now? I prayed that he was all right. And then there was someone beside me. I didn't know who it was. A young woman. She held my hand, right there as they tried to save him. She held my hand and said nothing. I was crying, I know, telling her that it was my first day at my new job, there at city hall. It was all over, everything, my dreams and plans. And the snow fell, and she held my hand and listened to my sorrow and grief, my regrets and my anguish to know that it was my fault. I didn't want to be late. How could I tell my parents what I had done? They were so proud of me. I had ruined it all.

The emergency crews were not so frantic now. They removed him from under the truck, placed him on a stretcher and covered him with a blanket, then put him in the ambulance, which left without its siren or flashing lights — just pulled up to the intersection and turned with the other traffic. It came upon me with certainty that I had killed a young man. A policeman asked me to come with him. He put me in the backseat of his police car. I looked back to the young woman through the window. She was walking away. I could see her hair in wet strands down her neck. I wanted her to turn to me so that I could see her. Then she was gone, lost in the snow.

At the station, the police managed to contact my father, who they said would come with a tow truck from his garage. I couldn't drive. I wasn't thinking of my new job. It was most likely gone. Everything had changed now. After an eternity sitting there with the knowledge of what I had done, my father arrived and talked to the policeman. There were to be no charges. Weather conditions, the policeman said. My father hooked up the truck and I got into the cab of the tow truck. I was relieved that he was with me. But he said nothing. I remember his hard mouth and silence. I wanted him to say something. But I suppose he knew that words could not accommodate a moment when someone had died. I was going home, having never made it to work: a failure in everyone's eyes, having killed someone for no reason. I felt like a monster.

Finally my father turned to me as we crossed the Oak Street Bridge. "Sometimes a terrible thing will happen," he said, "even when we have no intention for it to happen. But still we have to live with it."

That was all he said about that day. Later, my mother confided in me that the war had quieted him. "He had seen things and done things," she said with a grave sensibility.

A few days later, I learned that the City Clerk saved my job for me. I would begin again after Christmas. But Christmas was a miserable time for my family. A dismal pall hung about the house, dulling every pleasure. I wouldn't allow myself a laugh or a smile. The mind does not let go of something so shocking. Perhaps time could heal even that, although I had doubts about what it would mean to get over it, as if it were a disease to be rid of, an ailment awaiting a remedy.

The young man's name was Martin Rouse. I read about the accident in the newspaper: PEDESTRIAN STRUCK AT CAMBIE AND TWELFTH. But it was no accident. I did it all on my own. Sometimes people told me it was an accident, that no one was to blame. But I knew better. I couldn't stop thinking about him, his life, what things he had done and what would never come. I had seen his eyes through the falling snow. He had looked right into mine. That split second of life and death. And he had a family, a mother and father, a brother and sister. I took him away from them. Needing to say that I was sorry, I found their address and wrote them a letter. I never told anyone. But the letter returned unopened. They knew who I was.

Dear Mr. and Mrs. Rouse,

I know you must hurt all the time. You might not want to hear from me. I don't blame you. I just want to say that I'm sorry for what I did. It was snowing hard that day. Visibility was poor. But I was in a hurry. I didn't want to be late for work. It was supposed to be my first day on the job at city hall. But things went all wrong. I don't expect forgiveness. I just wanted to tell you how sorry I am for taking your son away from you. He never did anything wrong. It was my fault. There's nothing I can do to change it. I would if I could. I'm so sorry.

Yours truly,
Reuben Dale

I wanted to send the letter back to them. I couldn't just leave it alone, so I checked the address to be sure and re-mailed it. That time it never came back.

I finally made it to city hall and was welcomed in a quiet way by a sympathetic group of people. They spoke softly to me, their movements measured, gentle. They understood my fragility because I suppose they imagined their own. But still I could see it in their eyes, always aware of what I had done, never a separation from it, as if there were a shadow clinging to me that merged with my identity and became part of me. I was so relieved to have a routine, something else to distract me. But when I momentarily forgot Martin Rouse, I felt bad for not thinking of him. Somehow not to think of him would be to abandon him. So I kept him alive. I knew nothing about him except that he played the saxophone, perhaps in a school band or his own group. At lunch when I was out for my walks, I would pause along the curb and leave a prayer for him. There would always be someone watching from the tall windows.

Then in early February the telephone rang at my desk. The front office told me that there was someone to see me. It was a busy office with so much preparation for the mayor and aldermen: agendas and reports, public-hearing notices. There was always someone at the counter wanting information. And at that point in my career, I was the gofer, the new kid.

I knew right away she did not have a question about bylaws or committees. No, but she did have a question.

"How are you?" she asked me.

"Okay," I said.

"I'm a student. I was on my way to UBC that morning."

"Thanks," I said to her.

"For what?"

"Just being there."

"My name is June," she said.

"Reuben," I said dumbly.

"I know who you are," she laughed.

To see the caring that lit up in her face, in her eyes. There was something in her that could overcome anything. I just knew it. She had her hands on the counter, folded like a prayer. I wanted to touch them, feel her again. My hands moved, unconsciously, deliberately. I imagined her taking them, holding them. And yes, it was June that morning, as I sat in the police car, June who went into city hall to see the City Clerk to tell him about a tragic morning in the snow.

How a kid named Jonas made me remember Martin Rouse. I had forgotten him for a time; for there was no room for him. My misery nudged him out, but he wasn't far after all. He was just waiting for his cue as he always had, the lament of a saxophone, an old pickup truck, a siren in the distance, or a young man the same age with a certain look in his eyes that seemed to know something about me. Blamed me. And of course his name, "Martin," leading to my obsessive inquiry: Martin Luther King, Dean Martin, Ricky Martin, Aston Martin, Steve Martin, Martin Short, Martin Scorsese, purple martin. And then "Rouse" for the red-haired Anglo-Saxon invaders, with the Old French *rous* translating to *red* and the similar spelling, *rouse*. My God, did he have red hair? And with that I found Martin Rouse everywhere.

Those instruments of association — hair triggers all — so that my mind would drift back, a free fall, until I landed on that day. June could always tell. She would take my hand and gently say, "Let it go, Reuben," and Martin would fade away, for a little while at least. I needed her now, the drug of her reassurance.

The Closet

⌒

THE MORNINGS WERE HARD for me. It seemed that after I awoke, there was always that moment when a dream dissolves and a new day begins, the confusion of realities. But now the nightmares that belonged to the night would not disappear. I looked over and there was only a flat emptiness. I reached out with my arm and swept the space that had always kept her. Her breathing and the rise and fall of her chest. Sometimes when we slept in on weekends, I would wake first and watch her. It was the only time that she wasn't preparing or planning. She was in constant motion.

I made the bed, got dressed and stumbled down the hall to the kitchen. I could hear the rain on the aluminum patio cover. I opened the blinds to a dreary world. The swing of an empty bird feeder that the birds had given up on, and leaves covering the ground, the end of their glory, their season. Nothing lasts. I sat at the kitchen table and had a bowl of fruit and yogurt. It was easier. It wasn't long before the silence began its urgency. June was not there to approve of my progress, monitor my every consideration, my anxious thoughts and keep me straight and true with her ordered sensibility. What would she say about the pills I kept in my pocket, which my fingers searched for and my tongue held like candy that delivered such relief from this unkind and unending purgatory? *Oh, Reuben*, she would have said. And I would have put them away.

In the utter aloneness, there was something that I had never imagined or realized in my entire life. Not an ambition or aim, but still it seemed selfish somehow. I could decide what I wanted to do. There was no other to consider. Oh, of course there was the greater responsibility of a human being, but there in that house, there was no one to please. Everything was where I put it, how I left it. I could choose. It was raining with a bitter wind coming off the Salish Sea, and I could stay home awhile longer, to be alone in a room. I could take a book from one of the bookcases built into the wall on each side of the fireplace, maybe two or three, or one of the old first edition collectibles like Hemingway's *The Sun Also Rises* or older still, Conan Doyle's *The Lost World* and sit by the fire and make a day of it. Nothing to explain.

But it unnerved me to decide for myself; I did not have the confidence to do something on my own. There was one thing: the sympathy cards on the dining room table were like a walled village of tears. I had placed them around the flowers, now long gone. I read them all, the lovely hand writing, from friends, June's mostly, other teachers and her family from Calgary who, I was certain, would never speak to me again. June's sister wanted her buried with their mother and father in a cemetery by the Bow River. "No," I had to tell her, "that's not what June wanted." Then a thick silence. And a card from Vancouver City Hall — signed by everyone in the Clerks Department. I knew each one, how they wrote their names, signatures so individual, across and diagonal in every space and margin, the cramped blue strokes of a ballpoint pen.

The sentiments were kind. *You are always in our thoughts, sorry for your loss*, addressed to *Reuben and family*, a shocking omission, and then notes to me, *Reuben, please call if you need anything at all*. Walter and Lyle never came to the funeral, estranged brothers now it seemed. Just a card from them, and not in their own hand. It seemed to say that they would never call me. But why was that, I wanted to know, that I had to call them? How could I, really? *Oh, hi, this is Reuben. Well, I just wanted to tell you that life is hell and I feel like shit. I'm all alone and some kid has been following me, and my only friend is a scruffy sea dog who thinks the sun always shines on the Sunshine Coast. And I can't forget my doctor. At first I couldn't get one — the waiting lists, you know. But because he attended June in Emergency — she was already dead — I have a doctor. Too much information? Well, my doctor is a nice man, kind and sympathetic. He gave me some support in a little bottle. No, not Scotch. God, do you know what I'm saying? No one told me that life actually does not get better. It can turn on you like a savage dog. I can't piss now without June. I thought I would just call you. You asked me. I just thought that I would tell you that I am going to kill myself. I don't know how. Maybe I will walk myself to death. Why not?*

I cleared the cards from the table, all the butterflies and angels embossed in gold. It felt disrespectful somehow, to put them away, as if to do so meant that I had stopped caring, that a death was over and grief had to be cleared away. I placed them in a box. I couldn't throw them away. I suppose that it is human not to want to let go, to hold onto precious things, to give them life by our attention, our emotional attachment. They are just things after all, but perhaps they still have a quality of aliveness that belongs to the sensory world outside what we know. Sentiments spring to life in our eyes, on our lips. We hear the characters in a book when it is opened. As if they await our invitation like a musical greeting card. *You imagine a thing into existence*, June once said. I always believed her when she said something like that, her unswerving authority. But I was unprepared to discard anything that held some meaning of her life, even her death. All that belonged to her belonged to me now.

It was time to go out. I had survived the unease of my own presence. So much of my life was never a singular affair. I lived in a certain bound proximity to June. A kind of union that was more than a marriage, a shocking dependency that left me so unprepared for the basic things. I walked in my world, half a man and the other part of me entombed. It seemed the more I became aware of such things, the more awkward and estranged the world became. I did not trust myself. Even at city hall it was not confidence that helped me rise up through the ranks. Fear was my master and I obeyed it. It was a narrow journey, and I managed a career in the smallest of margins, knowing my limits, working hard within them, imitating self-assurance, mimicking independence and aplomb. I became an expert in my field, never complaining, never an unkind word. No one knew how afraid I was. I drifted away from every social affair and gathering, anywhere that I might make a friend. And when I did meet someone I liked, and a friendship was a possibility, I would retreat. Oh, the dread that someone would find out the truth about me. Although June knew that from the very first day, she still remained at my side, never wavering. It seems so impossible now, that kind of devotion.

I needed to put on a sweater and went to the bedroom. I stood before my closet and looked into the mirrored sliding door, to June's behind me. I thought about it often, to open it. But it had a seal. It was if it had taken on sacredness, an inviolable space that could not be entered or transgressed. Sometimes the temptation was too much. It was the closet where I could revive her with those tangible things in my hands. I went to the nightstand and turned over her picture. I returned to the closet and opened it slowly, clandestine and oddly discreet, the slide of the door revealing the clothes that she wore, an unsubstantial collage of muted tones. I turned on the closet light. And it was the smell before the feel of them, her perfume inked into the fabric. Her unique signature aroused in me such immediacy that I took them down off their hangers, one by one, and laid them on the bed, the suits she had worn to school, the skirts and blouses and sweaters, plumb and teal and navy and plaids, the tartan of the Royal Stewart. I was nervous about what I was doing, touching her things, lifting them up to my face to inhale them, to catch the fine bits of her woven there.

And then I lost my sense of what I was doing and went to her dresser and pulled open a drawer, and there were her finer things. I took them in my hands and rubbed them between my fingers. Things that I touched can scarcely be said, holding her negligee that was a distant memory, touching her bra that held her breasts. It was a shameful intimacy. I felt bad for what I was doing. It seemed perverse to seek pleasure in her clothes, to lie on top of them, to be with them, as if some pagan thing to bring her back. But these were losses in my life, my regrets and sorrows, the sensual deficits of a man. And then I stood up and looked at what I had done in the desperation to feel her once again. Her scattered clothes ruffled and pawed by a fool, to think that I held her panties in my hands. A word never uttered, a blasphemous affront to masculinity. And such a shock to me, the vulgar arousal. I wept like a baby until I caught myself in the mirror. I hated him, what he had become. To be moved now by dead things that held the throb of her life. I put all the clothes back and returned the other things to the dresser, unspeakable now, everything out of sight, hidden away.

Suddenly I felt a new urgency, remembering that Lori and Mandy needed a father, a whole father. But I could not call them, encourage them, soothe them in the way that their mother did. I never did a thing really, always handing over the telephone to June. Such visceral humiliation to see oneself in a mirror and know that your daughters were waiting, waiting for your resurrection.

I went to the kitchen to check the answering machine. I was so afraid to hear them, their voices. Isolation and loneliness were all I knew. But they needed some wisdom that I had, and I ached for redemption for my sinful fingers in the closet.

Dad, it's Lori, call me.

Dad, it's Lori. How are you? Call me.

Dad, please call.

Dad, we can't make it for Christmas. Exams and stuff.

Dad, it's Mandy. Are you coming for Christmas?

Dad, it's Lori. I'm going to Sean's parents for Christmas. They want you to come. Bye.

Dad, it's Mandy. I'm coming out there if you don't call.

Dad, we're worried about you. What's going on?

Acts of Grief

❧

I THREW ON A SWEATER. I had to get away from the house, but the rain beat wildly against the panes, relentless now with a temper to flush me out into the world, raw and naked. I took the Subaru and parked in the marina lot and fought what seemed a gale all the way down to the marina store. I had to heave on the door. It seemed that someone had nailed it shut. And when I finally got it open, I couldn't close it. The howling in my ears and the spray up from the beach crashed over the dock and soaked the back of my legs.

"Come on now, put some muscle into it!" Nelson shouted from inside.

I managed to get in and closed the door behind me. "Those hinges could use some oil," I said.

"Oh, never mind that," Nelson said. "Hang up your dripping hat and coat. I'll get your coffee. I knew you'd be back."

"Admiral, sir," I said, "that would be great."

"What's your point with the name?"

"You know, Admiral Nelson and the sea," I said playing along with what I thought was his amusement with names.

"Oh yeah, I get your meaning there, Reuben. One-armed master of the sea. It's good to see you again."

I stood there a moment as he went into the back for my coffee. He was a curious sort for sure, but there was something about Nelson that made me feel untroubled. And it was good to sit at the table near the stove blazing away in warm simulation with the weather having fits and the flashing banging outside the window.

Nelson set my coffee cup down — another whale navigating the sides.

"Heck of a spell of rain," he said. "Sally said she's never seen a No-vember so squally. There's a boat I need to take out and store in the yard. Just sit tight there, Reuben, I won't be long. It's a Trophy, a good fishing boat. I'll take it in on a trailer. Store it proper when the weather breaks."

"I've got nowhere else to go," I said thoughtlessly. Then I checked myself. "I didn't mean it that way."

"No worries," Nelson said. "I've got to keep moving myself. Don't know what I would do without this place."

"It must keep you busy."

"A man needs to work," he said. "He needs to know that he matters. He needs a reason to get up every day and be happy about it."

"I guess I had that. But I thought I had worked enough. June left her school so we could retire together. That's all that seemed to matter. I wasn't worried about what I would do."

"At least you had a summer together."

Then an awkward silence fell between us. I could feel him looking down at me. He didn't seem to mind the suspension of our conversation. And it would appear that he was comfortable with any topic. I liked Nelson Grommet. He was an honest, unpretentious man who seemed to understand that not everyone was as fearless as he was. Then he broke away and left out the back door.

I turned to watch him along the boat ramp with that miserable squall up his back. There was something about being near the water that satisfied my restlessness. There was so much life there, constant motion, a certain violent meeting of the sea. A force lived within it that bashed against anything in its way, a recklessness that seemed intent to devour the land. But I was safe with my coffee, cradling the mug in my hands, as Nelson walked the boat along the dock and secured a line to a winch. He blew on his hands as he worked. The wind whipped across the marina, the building groaning and shivering, a show unlike anything that you might pay to see. All that and still the gulls found some pleasure wheeling in great arcs. My eyes followed them at their play. How they would suddenly stop, suspended and tilting like kites. And then a presence by the door. My heart dropped like a stone to see him standing there, unheard in the riot of wind, the kid staring right into me.

Uncertain of his motives, what it was that he wanted, I couldn't find the words to address him. Although nothing had changed, it gave me chills to see those accusing eyes again. But it was clear that he had come to see me, down through the driving rain to tell me at last what his business was. He glanced out the window; perhaps measuring how long Nelson would be away from the store. Then he walked slowly to my table.

"Can I sit down?" he asked.

"All right," I said. He sat down, placing his hands on the table, and leaned toward me.

"Look," he said, "I'm having a hard time with all this."

"All what?"

"That Mrs. Dale died." He looked away just then.

"Mrs. Dale?"

"Yeah, she was my teacher." He met me now. I could see that he struggled to speak with me.

"Really?" I wanted to know more now.

"At Royal Academy."

"So why are you here?"

"I don't know."

He kept looking away, changing positions, his long legs cumbersome, awkward. Then a hand would sweep through his hair and he would sit up. Unsuited for a chair.

"The funeral was three months ago," I said.

"I know."

"So you came from Vancouver to do what?"

"Hey man, I thought you might get all weird."

"Why wouldn't I? You've been sneaking around here for a week."

"You don't know anything about me."

"I don't want to know anything about you."

"She made a difference."

"She made a difference?"

"Yeah, you know — a flunking kid and all that shit."

"Tell me."

"I was failing English. I hated it. I wasn't going to graduate and I didn't care."

"She was a good teacher. I know that."

"Yeah, but it didn't matter. I didn't want to be in her class. She told these dumb stories about her boat. She made up poems about it. She had the class create these scenes, different scenes and outcomes with the boat. She had a picture of it. And then something happened; I kind of got it: what the imagination can do. She turned me on to poetry, to writing. She inspired me. I began to dream of sailing. It was amazing. She was amazing. She helped me graduate. I would have given up if it wasn't for her. That's all. I couldn't believe it when I heard."

"She talked about the boat?"

"All the kids loved to hear about it. The adventures of *my June*."

"You knew the name."

"Yeah."

"You knew where to come?"

"Everyone knew where she was going."

"Yes, there were students at the funeral. Some from a long time ago."

"I couldn't."

"So you came to pay your respects?"

"Yeah."

"You'll be going back then."

"Didn't you ever have a teacher who made a difference in your life?"

He had no idea. "Sure," I said.

"I thought if I saw the boat, then I would be all right. It would make it easier."

"Yes, well you've seen it."

"You don't like me."

"I don't care one way or the other."

"I had this crazy idea that you would show it to me, take me out or something. I heard so much about the boat. It was like a legend. She made it seem like something from a fable."

"Why would I do that?"

"I don't know."

"You don't know me."

"Yeah, whatever."

"Look, kid . . ."

"It's Jonas."

"Jonas, I think it's time for you to go home."

"You're right. I'm sorry. I'm leaving in a few days. I just wasn't . . ."

"Wasn't what?"

"I wasn't counting on you being an asshole."

"What?"

"I thought you'd be different."

"I don't believe this."

"I thought you'd be like her."

I sat there unable to speak. How he glared with such bold intensity. I felt like a child rebuked, with a welt on my cheek where he scorched me with his hand. He stood up and made his way to the front door as Nelson was coming in through the back.

"She would have helped me," he said turning with his hand at the door. "The way she cared about . . . forget it. Just forget it." Then he was gone.

Nelson came in, drying his hair with a towel. I managed to reach into my pocket for one of my pills. I was frantic to open the container under the table.

"It's letting up now," he said. "She's all but blown herself out."

I just looked at him. He leaned over the counter, all red-faced from the cold and wet, his hair a frightful mop. But all I could think of was the kid. He was clearly upset. I wasn't prepared to hear sorrow turn into resentment.

"So what's going on with you, Reuben?" Nelson asked.

"Nothing," I said.

"You're looking a mite peaked. Coffee's not that bad, is it?"

"No, it's not that. That kid was just here."

"The one you chased up the hill?"

"Yes, that same kid. He just walked in here and sat down."

"Son of a bitch," Nelson said, "never would have thought it." He wrapped the towel around his neck like a prizefighter.

"He was one of June's students. His name is Jonas."

"There you go, Reuben. That mystery's solved."

"He'll be going back to Vancouver soon."

"So why the interest in the boat?"

"It seems she told her class all about it, the legend of *my June*. School stuff. He just wanted to see it. He thought I would show it to him. He wants to sail. I guess he's just trying to sort things out for himself."

"I had a crush on my tenth-grade teacher," Nelson said. "I thought she was the most beautiful woman I had ever seen. Her name was Miss Peach. I was going to marry her until I found out she got married. Well, she had always been just Miss Peach. It never occurred to me that she might get married one day. I damn near quit school. I was so broken-hearted."

"You think he might have had a crush on June?"

"I'm just sayin', Reuben. No one can be sure of these things. It could be that he had his heart broken."

"I don't know about that."

"He's really got you rattled."

"I'll be glad when he's gone."

"Have you heard about the ripple effect?"

I drew a blank. "You mean like a stone in a pond?"

"When something happens, there's an effect — the ripples. Well they can go on and on. There's no telling what can happen from that one thing. I've seen it myself. Miss Peach, she started it all. I can't say for sure what came first. I had pneumonia and missed a lot of school. She came to the house in the early summer to see how I was. It was my birthday as it turned out, the Fourth of July, if you can believe it. She had a book for me. *Moby Dick*. Now was it the pneumonia or the book? I don't know. But I can tell you that I read the book and I wanted to go to sea and I wanted to see whales.

"And I did just that, left for Seattle when I was old enough, ten years after the war. Before we bought this place. I got a job on a freighter, up the coast to Alaska and then joined the crew on a Canadian Pacific steamship. I saw whales and I saw the sea. And then wouldn't you know it, I became a certified seaman and signed on for the summer on a Wind-class icebreaker, the CCGS *Labrador*, bound for research off Ellesmere Island in the Arctic Ocean. It was 1964, and we navigated the most northern position of any Canadian ship. And that's when I saw them, narwhals, blowing with their ten-foot tusks. I'll never forget it. You wouldn't believe me if I told you Sally was a mate on that same ship, standing on the deck beside me loving them whales.

"And I've had a life on the sea, and by the sea, and all the whales I could count. See the poster there on the wall: *National Geographic's* "Whales of the World." And you know, the ripples aren't done yet. There was a grey whale in the strait last summer. Come to see me, I like to think. A whole life that would never have been. I think it was Miss Peach who did it. You get my meaning, Reuben? What stone did your wife throw down for that boy? We don't know. I'm just saying. All because of a book. I wish I still had it. Left it behind in our old house along the Mississippi. That was in 1955."

"That's a curious theory, Nelson," I said. Such astonishing things he would say, a story stretching back into the past, but a certain richness to it all, a life that he loved . . . *a reason to get up every day and be happy about it*.

"It's no theory, Reuben," Nelson said soberly.

I couldn't tell him what wore on me sitting there. *my June* adrift without me, not knowing how I could once again feel the weight of her against the sea. I was afraid to sail on my own. And a stone cast to sow a young man's dream? There was nothing I could do for Jonas. No, I couldn't ask Nelson for advice, not so soon. I knew what he would say and kept the question away from him, held it away from the answer. He would reach into the bag of his lore and find a sailor's verse, exact for my troubles like a witch with her cures.

Boundary Bay

✧

THE RIPPLES FOUND ME on every shore. They reached for the innocent without malice or beneficence, but as something that began, touching
things, changing the unnameable moments of life that were overlooked,
too small to be noticed. And they spread further still and claimed another
victim, but now with bitterness and wrath, all connected to that one instant at Cambie and Twelfth.

Early March in South Delta and the brant were in at Boundary Bay
— low black lines settling over the shallow sea, staging now and soon
moving north to the Arctic coasts to nest along the tundra pools. And the
hunters were ready in their driftwood shacks spaced above the high-
water mark as they did as long as my father could remember. He had his
own makeshift shack of plywood that Walter and Lyle had dragged
along the dyke before the season began when the sun leaked out its first
impression behind Mount Baker. The choice spots were scarce, and they

were determined to have first pick. The flocks were not what they used to be, my father told me on the telephone.

"Over-hunting," he said, "and it saddens me to tell it."

Those winter Sundays when the garage was closed, my father would steal out into the dark with his shotgun. Walter and Lyle, so similar to him in their habits and work, would go with him, carrying their own grease smell and pump-action Brownings. Hunting never appealed to me, killing things like that. I couldn't sit in a blind, shivering for hours, smoking cigarettes, waiting for the first flights of brant, then rear up with the cold barrels choked and primed to bring them down unaware.

But I will admit my jealousy for the things they shared, the simple talk that moved them, the humour and laughter of things remembered. I always felt outside of their community. They were like brothers, my father and his sons. And I grew more estranged, as if I had lost that bond of family, of fellowship and alliance, something guaranteed always to be the way you left it. But still I had my greatest ally, my mother. She knew the depths of me, accepted who I was. My never-failing champion. But her eyes revealed to me her sorrow; not for her station in life, the selfless work of a housewife, the sacrifice, but because of what lived inside me. A mother always wishes for the essential, happiness for her children.

I wanted to be a part of their hunting fraternity just once, not to participate in the ritual of men with guns, but to be present with them so that perhaps I could look back and say, *yes, I was there with you. Do you remember that day?* I left my apartment in Kerrisdale when the streets were black and empty, and June was just a possibility. It was the last Sunday of brant season, and I was feeling anxious. I was always nervous in the mornings when the day was new and my sensitivities were raw and unfamiliar, as if I doubted my place in the world, worried that I could not handle the responsibilities of my new job, my life. It seemed my perceptions were forever altered that day. I would never see in the same way again. I would see the world through the lens of fear.

They were waiting in the driveway in Walter's four-wheel-drive carryall under a cloud of exhaust. They greeted me well enough, and I could see that my father was pleased to have all his sons together for such a display of masculinity — to him at least, where a man had a proper and estimable role in life. I knew he believed that it would do me good to dress down in a mackinaw and go unshaven for a day. Walter drove and our father sat in the front seat beside him. I sat with Lyle in the back, leaning forward, listening to the talk of brant hunters, a shot they made the week before, the misses, the red brand of my father's cigarette punctuating such inflated but delightful storytelling.

Lyle just smiled at such recounting. He was not a boastful young man, but eager to listen to those in his company and offer a groan or a laugh. Always in good humour, he never hesitated to tease me about my city life. It wasn't always about cars and hunting. He knew a world existed outside of Ladner, away from the farmland and river. He was the middle brother, closest to my age. We never fought growing up, did not come to blows over possessions or opinions, the way he did with Walter who thought it his right and duty as the eldest. And I could see then how Walter would look at him, what seemed like regret for tormenting him those years before. That may have been true but there was more. It truly grieved him to know that Lyle had grown restless and had plans beyond fixing flats and the endless *fill'er-ups*. They had been inseparable, bound by some unwritten contract to the garage, to our father and his work. An admirable loyalty that now seemed as if it would not endure. Lyle's ribbing about my suit and tie was just his inquiry, his testing of the waters, for something else. I knew there was a girl somewhere. There had to be. He was just that happy.

We parked at the dyke in the pre-dawn. There were other cars and trucks, hunters already in their blinds, an anxiety among sportsmen to be first along stream or shore. Shotguns were slipped from their cases and boxes of shells stuffed into pockets. A sack of decoys and hip waders, and thermoses and sandwiches handed to me in a rucksack. All was ready and we set off down the dyke, following the curve of the bay, smoking in the cool dusk and quiet with our own thoughts. The mood was spirited, expectant. I always knew when my father was happy. It would come in the most unusual of ways. He would offer a timely fart for us all to consider, and then turn around and blame me, the youngest. There would be the predictable moans and objections and shoves. It was his way of communicating his affections, a most indelicate but loving act.

We broke away from the dyke and followed a sand trail. The blind was just a shadow, a shape to hide us. Driftwood piled against the plywood shell, camouflaged, something of geometry heaved from the sea. Inside the blind we leant the shotguns against a wall in readiness, below a window overlooking the bay. The tide was up. I tucked the thermoses and lunches in a corner. Walter pulled on his hip waders and set the string of decoys out in the water. They floated stiff but looked real enough, rising and falling in the gentle waves coming into the beach. Then we all found stools from blocks of wood and sat and smoked and waited for the sun. After a while my father whispered to me. "Walter thinks he's a better shot than Lyle."

"I don't *think* it," Walter said.

"I always let a few go," Lyle said.

Walter laughed.

"Reuben, how about that coffee?" our father said. I knew he was smiling.

I removed the thermoses and cups and poured coffee for everyone. Silence for a moment as the hot coffee approached our lips, then a cigarette, and a certain contentment in that simple ceremony. It seemed life was good just then. There was nothing else. At that moment it was clear to me why they hunted. It wasn't just shooting, sharing smokes and coffee. It wasn't just bringing home birds for our mother to pluck and her playful complaints. It was all of those things as if it were something on its own. It was a tangible promise that such moments would sustain them for the rest of their lives.

When the sun finally rose over the bay, and the sweet spring smells crept out of the hardhack and willows behind us, the black flights with their throaty *cronks* came sweeping in. There was a blast down the beach and another and another. I stood back as the shotguns came up before me and sounded a succession of explosions, with birds falling into the sea. Then silence, and the flocks veering away, with others drawing near. And once again the three of them taking their turn. The smell of gunpowder and heated barrels, the smell of men in their cherished and worn-out clothes. And still I was distant, an observer, spectator. But I would settle for that, to be with them, near them.

After the birds were lifted from the water, there was great boasting around the blind. We stood around and admired them, their feathers, and a seamless blackness over the front and back, the white thumbprint on the neck. It was early still, and we stood back in the sun. The distant blasts began to slacken. And then one that was close. It was loud, a detonation. And how odd to see Lyle suddenly pitch forward as if knocked from behind. It seemed that he had tripped but he stayed down on his knees. Our father looked at him, and Walter reached down with his hand to help him to his feet.

"Come on, Lyle get up," he said thinking it was one of Lyle's pranks.

But Lyle did not move, and then I could see it, the dark stain of blood radiating from the back of his right leg behind the knee. "Christ, he's bleeding!" I shouted. And our father at once knelt down to see what it was, how it could be true.

"My God, he's been shot!" he said.

Walter searched around the blind, checked the shotguns that were idle against the wall. Then he looked about and hurried down the trail to the blind that was closest to us. And then he came rushing back. "No one there," he said. "What's going on, Dad?"

Lyle was face down now and our father reached around him and unfastened his belt and pulled down his bloodied pants, and there, a black hole and burping blood. He gasped as we all gasped. Although Lyle made no sound and did not move, I could see the flutter of his eyes. He was alive at least. And then our father seized his own belt and turned to Walter, his eyes like stones.

"Walter," he said, "take the belt and tie it above the wound and cinch it tight. Then give me your shirt. We have to stop the bleeding. Hurry now!" Then he turned to me. "Reuben, get out to the clubhouse at the golf course. Call an ambulance!"

"What the hell happened?" I said. The blood coming still and percolating onto the sand as Walter worked frantically with the belt on Lyle's thigh.

"Go now, Reuben. Run!" he said, his face awash with such urgency. Archie Dale, who *had seen things and done things in the war*, the blood of his second son on his hands, a blessed father who knew what to do.

I spun there in the sand and ran down the trail toward the dyke. I could see the blood still, with Lyle falling and something before, a queer sense I could not explain. The sand was soft and my footing laboured. I felt heavy, restrained. I wanted to be free of it, and then at last I reached the dyke. It was solid and propelled me on, gravel spitting from my footfall. I willed my legs to outrun the flow of blood. A little faster now. *Poor Lyle*. It was all I could think about. *Poor Lyle*. I ran swift and true toward the road. The golf course was just across the road from Walter's truck.

Then something entered my vision — down below me across a wide ditch, someone running through the willows, ducking, stumbling. We ran together, side by side but separated from the slough. It was a strange thing to see, a young man running like that, a young man trying to get away. Something was wrong.

"Hey!" I shouted at him. He didn't look my way, so determined he was to get free of the brush, to get somewhere. And still my legs under me, inexhaustible. I shouted again, trying to see what he looked like. I wanted him to turn to me, to see his face, his height and build, his light red hair. Then the road came up, and he disappeared where the slough veered away toward a culvert. I couldn't stop. I couldn't follow him.

I made the clubhouse. The manager called an ambulance and the police. I waited for them and soon could hear the sirens and flashing lights coming down 12th Avenue toward Boundary Bay Road. Oh, that eerie similarity. I just prayed they would get to Lyle in time. And they did. He nearly bled to death there in the sand. His right knee was shot out but he wouldn't die, although he would never walk the same again. After that day my father would never hunt again, never pick up a gun.

The police caught Donny Rouse on the freeway racing through Richmond. They found his father's hunting rifle in the bush one hundred feet behind our blind. They told us afterward that Donny Rouse had made many trips to Ladner. He had asked around. He wanted know all about the Dales: where they went and what they did. He staked out our house, and he also watched the blind from his hiding place on those many Sundays. He ate his lunch there as he prepared his plan. Perhaps it was there that he decided that it would be Lyle. But there was one thing he had not prepared for; he had never shot a rifle before that day. It was that omission, perhaps, that saved Lyle's life.

Before sentencing, the only thing Donny Rouse told the court was that he wanted Reuben Dale to know what it felt like to lose a brother. I had an unusual reaction to that news, not the outrage of our family and the community, not condemnation for hurting my brother, for forever changing his life. No, I didn't hate Donny Rose for what he did. I could almost understand it, as if that too, was part of my own creation, stretching outwards, a reckless and uncontrollable thing.

Donny Rouse was sentenced to seven years in the Matsqui Penitentiary.

Snow Falling
from Heaven

THE SNOW CAME SOFTLY, intermittent. There was no wind or breeze and the flakes fell straight down like blessings. I sat at my kitchen table and watched them. I had filled the feeder with sunflower seeds so that the sparrows and rosy finches would gather there, little bundles of life. I was sorry to have left it unattended for so long. The world was not so bleak just then. Heavy snow was in the forecast and I knew that it would give me trouble. It was December 1st and Seaside was preparing for the annual "Christmas Light Up." I would go down there later, stroll along the pretty streets to see the lights. Just the thought of Christmas made me think of the girls.

Lori and Mandy shared an apartment. They would be home from school by now. Maybe they would be out with friends or perhaps they would be having their dinner. I didn't want to bother them. They had busy lives, term finals, I imagined. They would need to study. So much to do in Toronto. How I could come up with the excuses, the avoidance. June never would have allowed it. What would she be thinking? There was so much shame in me, as if I had failed the world, even that kid, Jonas. I didn't want to let her down. I had to do something; I couldn't continue to ignore them. They didn't deserve another moment's selfishness.

Like a coward, I took a tranquilizer and stood at the window holding the telephone and watching the birds at the feeder, listening to the rings across the country.

"Hello."

"Lori, it's Dad."

"Who?"

"Smart ass."

"We were just about to call the police!"

"That bad?"

"That bad."

"Sorry about that."

"We worry about you. You know?"

"I know."

"Thanks for calling."

"So how are you?"

"It's crazy right now."

"Thought so."

"Dad, can you come out for Christmas?"

"Don't think so, Lori. Not this year. I was hoping you and Mandy would come out to Seaside."

"You know we would love to, Dad, but there's just too much going on."

"I know. How's that boyfriend of yours?"

"Sean, he's such a good guy. He's brilliant. You're going to love him."

"What about Mandy?"

"Well . . . she's out with a friend."

"Christmas will be hard this year."

"It doesn't seem right . . . that Mom's gone."

"No."

"It's like an error. Someone made a mistake. She's just been misplaced and waiting for us to pick her up."

"I know what you mean."

"She always had an answer. Something to mend every little hurt."

"She did."

"Dad, how are you doing?"

"I'm doing all right. I'm a little lonely. But I walk every day, long walks."

"You need to be with people."

"I know."

"Have you made any new friends?"

"There's the owner of the marina. He seems like a pretty good guy."

"That's good."

"Then there's this kid, one of your mother's students. He claims that she helped him graduate. He came to see the boat."

"*my June?*"

"Yes."

"Oh, I remember Mom telling me something about that. She used it in one of her English classes."

"Well this kid thought I would show it to him. He wants to sail."

"So?"

"He's going back to Vancouver."

"He came all that way to see it for himself?"

"It seems so."

"Maybe he came because Mom inspired him. She did that a lot, you know. It was one of her gifts."

"Yes."

"So show him the boat. Take him sailing."

"I don't know, Lori."

"Mom would."

"Probably."

"She would. She would do anything to help someone. You know, give someone a leg up."

"That kid, I don't know him."

"Who knows, maybe it was Mom who sent him."

"Only if she knew that I would do it."

"How about . . . she sent him because she knew that you wouldn't do it?"

"Oh, she sent me a dragon to slay. I see."

"Just a push. You know Mom. To get you out there."

"Well, I don't think it's what I need right now."

"Okay."

"Where do you girls get ideas like that?"

"Our only limitations are the ones we place on ourselves. Isn't that what you used to say?"

"That was your mother."

"Whatever. It might do you good. Who knows?"

"All right, I better let you go. I'll call you soon. Give Mandy my love."

"Love you, Dad."

"Love you too."

"We'll come out in the summer, when schools over. We'll help you with Mom's things."

"All right."

"Bye."

It was such a wonderful and painful conversation, not quite real over the telephone but real enough to sustain me for a while. Lori shared her mother's fortifying persuasion, an indomitable spirit, a force that was fluid and moved effortlessly through them. It was in everything they did, formed part of their identity. And I was the beneficiary, always surrounded by such charitable energy. I lost mine some time ago, courage, shortchanged perhaps on the day I was born. I suppose there wasn't enough to go around just after the war. It had been all used up overseas. And Mandy, I wondered — what was going on with that girl?

As the snow continued falling and the dark came into the house, I turned on the lights. So now dinner for one: one pork chop, one potato, one carrot. It seemed pointless somehow to cook just for oneself. There was a certain attraction to skipping it, to avoid the pots and pans, perhaps eat out of a can, something frozen, a submarine sandwich from the gas station. I even thought that perhaps ice cream, chocolate, would be a good substitute for eating real food. But I saved that for really bad days, miserable days. I could hear them all, June and the girls, wagging a cautionary finger. And so a pork chop it was.

I finished my dinner and put on a heavy coat. I thought I would shovel the driveway. There was only an inch or two of snow but I figured it would easier to shovel a couple of inches than wait until there was a foot or more after I got home from Seaside's Light Up. I began to push the shovel down the driveway. As the snow fell, it seemed to whisper to me, to go back there. I pushed harder, and it wasn't long before my neighbour came over. His name was Bert.

"Hey there, Reuben," he said.

"Oh, hi, Bert," I said, as I stopped shovelling.

"What do you think of this stuff?" Bert said.

He wore a Winnipeg Jets toque pulled over his ears. The snow stuck to it like white burs. Bert was a large man, most would call him obese. It seemed that the flesh was sliding off his face. He always looked a bit grave and tired around his eyes. He had sold life insurance in Winnipeg and was forced to retire because of his health. He hadn't been around since June died.

"I don't mind it," I said, "if you don't have to drive."

"Yeah, I know what you mean." He was looking into my open garage.

"Are you going downtown tonight?"

"For the Light Up?"

"It might be something to see. I didn't see it last year."

"No, I guess you didn't," Bert said. He was sure curious about my garage.

"Are you putting up lights, Bert?"

"I put them on the shrubs. Fanny won't let me on the roof."

"I guess we have to be careful. We're getting on, you know." My sad humour.

"Say, Reuben, do you mind if I have a look at your shop?" he said a little sheepishly. I could see that the open garage door was distracting him.

"My shop?" I said.

"I always like to see the different set-ups. Some guys like to have the long bench with a vice and all the tools on pegboards. Then some have the whole garage filled with table saws, jigsaws and lathes and such. I've seen some that have stoves in there for the winter. And one of those little fridges to keep beer. I've heard them called man caves."

"Go ahead," I said, not following him in. I made a couple passes with the shovel before he came back out.

"Is your shop out back, Reuben?"

Bert, you live next door. Did you see a building in my back yard? "No, no shop back there, Bert."

"Oh, I thought you had a shop."

"No shop," I confessed. I had never talked to Bert much before, but I found myself in a brighter mood. It surprised me. "I have a hammer and three screwdrivers in a cupboard," I told him. "A Phillips, slot and Robertson. But I don't know which is which. They're just a star, slot and square to me. I might have the slot right. In fact they might be still locked up."

"Locked up?"

"You might have heard me cussing after we moved in, Bert." For some reason I found myself telling him the story. Perhaps it was just his company on a snowy night. "It wasn't pretty," I said. "I was putting up brackets for our new blinds. But every time I tried to turn the screw, it would fall on the floor. Then when I got it going, I would hit something hard and it wouldn't go in at all. Then the bracket would fall on the floor. Then the screwdriver. So I took a big nail and drove it through the hole in the bracket. But the nail bent. So I had to take the hammer and tried to pry it out, but it wouldn't come. So I just applied some leverage and the head of the hammer put a hole in the wall the size of a tennis ball. I had to call a drywaller. Lucky he was handy and put up the blinds. June thought I should turn over all my tools to the proper authority. She laughed so hard that day. We both did. It went from hell to heaven. Just her laughing like that. If you're wondering about it, I didn't feel bad in the least. June knew only the upside of things. Laughter was her remedy. It was one of our finest moments together."

Bert looked stunned for minute, trying to imagine his incapable neighbour with his tools locked up forever. "I make furniture for the grandchildren," he then said proudly. "I have all the gadgets. I love tools. I always wanted to do woodworking."

"Must be nice," I said.

"Do you play cards, Reuben?"

"No cards," I said.

"Golf?"

"Waste of a good walk."

"Bingo?"

"Bingo?"

"Over at the senior's centre."

"No bingo." I once told June that if she ever caught me playing bingo she had my permission to pummel me senseless. We had a pact that we wouldn't grow old in the conventional way. No beige polyester slacks for me. No small dog on my lap as I drove around town. No knitting afghans, or taking in ladies tea for June. Angela Lansbury's *Murder, She Wrote* was banned from the house. And *Jeopardy* — well, it would be too late.

"So what do you do to keep busy?"

"Well, I read and I walk."

Bert nodded. "My shop saves me some days, I can tell you, when I get in Fanny's . . ."

He looked horrified just then. "It's all right, Bert."

He looked up at the snow. It melted on his hot face. "I better get back in," he said. "Should be supper time. See you later, Reuben."

I watched Bert shuffle over to his house. He seemed like a big kid. I stood there in the snow, in the silence, the street lights pulsing endless flakes. He had come over just to ask me about my shop. And I spoke to him. Who would have known that a memory would be released like that, would bring her back to me? It was a gift from the big guy, hurting now because he forgot himself, a memory to shepherd me away, for a moment at least, from the snow falling on Cambie Street. The snow did not wish to punish me. It was frozen patterns after all, unlimited, perfect and incomparable. It was just snow.

A Thousand Voices

❧

I HAD GOOD WARM BOOTS and a coat with a hood, thick woollen mitts. And *I read and I walk*, I had told Bert. Not a full plate for retirement. But as I made my way down Dory Avenue in the snow, I was happy to walk, to listen to the nostalgic squeak of my boots. Cars passed heading toward Main Street. There were others walking too, children with their parents, stopping to scoop up handfuls of snow. Some were raising their faces to catch snowflakes on protruding tongues. Walking seemed a tonic for all that was urgent, all that assailed my peace of mind. My thoughts were clearer somehow, as if the movement of arms and legs brought things into alignment, a rhythm facilitating order. The body needed to move I had come to learn in those difficult months. What a strange but simple thing, going nowhere in particular, swinging my arms, keeping myself alive.

I came up to Mariner Street and could see how down at the marina the dock was strung with lights. People were coming from all directions. Music was playing, familiar carols, and snow falling still. The night was illumined and expectant. I turned downhill toward the town centre and could see that the trees in every yard were now shrouded in snow, branches and clotheslines bowed and thickening, and fences growing taller. Porch lights seemed to offer an invitation, a lamp in a window, a refuge. I slid on my feet like a child, a measured prudence in my daring, but pathetic I was sure, to the teens rushing by me with their immortal hearts.

It struck me just then, a longing to share the moment. I wanted so much to see the delight in June's eyes. It never really mattered to me if I failed to be moved by a song or a sunset. I had eyes of course and ears, but I had grown used to experiencing such things through her. I knew she looked forward to the Light Up, her dear Seaside dressing up for Christmas. She talked about it, things to look forward to, such as hot chocolate in the town square. Then all at once I felt sad. Memories, I knew, could turn a mood like a page. And to think I played there on that snowy hill in a moment's forgetting.

As I reached Main Street, I stayed on the periphery, looking across from the square in front of the town hall. I would just watch, nothing more. There was a tent set up with hot chocolate being served. I could see people milling down the street, waiting for the strike of seven o'clock on the big town clock. And then as the time approached, the mayor stepped up to a microphone on a platform bedecked with garlands and bows. Wearing a great fur coat and hat, he seemed a character borrowed from a Klondike carnival of old. The snow fell and it seemed that sadness could not last on such a night. There was a fire truck and a police car waiting their cue. Then the music stopped and the mayor tapped the microphone to begin the festivities.

"Thank you," he said, "to all the residents of Seaside for coming down to participate in the 25th annual Seaside Christmas Light Up. We are blessed by this first snowfall of the year." A great cheer erupted. "And thank you to all the volunteers and business owners who make this event possible. So without further delay, the countdown will begin."

As he counted down from ten, the children in the square joined in.

When the number one was reached, another chorus of cheers rose up and someone threw a switch. A blaze of lights sprang out of the dark and there seemed to be a thousand people in the street. The crowd parted as the fire truck and police car moved ahead, their lights flashing and the music playing once again. Trailing behind was an old Chevy truck restored to a brilliant red. In the back stood Santa Claus himself, who at once began to wave, while elves alongside tossed candy canes as the progression moved down Main Street.

The beauty of it all dazzled me, a town so remote now buzzing with an electric happiness that seemed to stir in my own chest. It was not joy that I felt, but a comfort that joy could still be found. It seemed hopeful. It was like a dream where the senses just follow, where nothing seems real and it didn't really matter. Some creation to counter the dark nights, as if the people of the town were jolly pagans of the solstice gathering around the winter fires.

Every business displayed their coloured lights around the windows and awnings, along the facades and eves, red, green, blue and yellow. Over the street were brightly lit banners fashioned into bells and holly, with icicles dripping white light. Wire frames of reindeer and snowmen were lit and mobile along the sidewalks with their stiff and cheery greetings. The lights bled out into the snow, falling upon the merry faces, making it seem a timeless affair, something magical cut out of the fabric of a good world. Then I heard someone calling to me from the square. I knew the voice. It was Nelson Grommet.

With the snow falling before my eyes I could not at first find him in the crowd. There were only shapes now, but I knew his shape. And then there he was standing by a fir tree decorated with lights. There was snow in his hair and his shoulders were white with it. He held a candle, and beside him was a woman in a wheelchair. I did not acknowledge her, as if she belonged to someone else and only waited there for her escort. In her lap a candle flickered against the snow.

"Good to see you, Reuben," Nelson said.

"I didn't think the Sunshine Coast got snow," I teased.

"Oh, enjoy it," he said. "The rain will wash it all away in the morning."

Then the woman raised her candle to me. "This is for you," she said.

I looked to Nelson, not understanding who or what was there before me.

"This is Sally," he said. "We come to the Light Up for another reason. The candles are provided by the Seaside Hospice to remember those we have lost. Well, we never forget. You know that."

I took the candle from her. She was so sweet and tiny in the chair. She wore a Nordic cap and a tartan blanket covered her legs. Her smile made you know at once that she was the kindest of souls. "Thank you," I said to her. They both knew who the candle was for. It was so thoughtful. And I forgot about the coloured lights. How meaning can shift so easily, seamlessly. But I found it difficult to ask them who they were remembering on that night. I felt awkward standing there fretting over my fears. I didn't want to know. I didn't want to hear a sad story just then. Wasn't holding a candle enough? But it was rude not to ask, inquire at least. Perhaps the name of a parent, or some acquaintance. That would not be so hard; I would nod and smile warmly. But it all seemed so shallow.

And then I asked. "Who are you remembering, Nelson?"

He looked at me as if he never expected the question. All at once his eyes became sad. He looked down at Sally. She reached up and took his hand. Such tenderness between them. I hadn't seen that in him as I sat at the little blue table overlooking the sea. He seemed so rough and somewhat whimsical, a salty dispenser of long-forgotten chronicles.

"Well, it's for our daughter," Sally said.

I was startled by the news of a child. I hadn't imagined that Nelson was a father. I never asked him, and I never asked about Sally. Not once did I wonder. "I didn't know," I said.

"Oh, it was a long time ago, Reuben," Sally said. "But we still think of our Emily all the time."

"I'm sorry," I said. The only words that would come just then. The how was left alone.

"It has been forty years now," she continued in spite of my anxiety. "Is that right, Nelson?"

"Forty years it is, Sal."

"A drunk driver," Sally said. "We were over in Courtenay for the day.

We were just heading back to the ferry in the afternoon, laughing one minute and then everything went blank. It happened so fast."

"It was a long time ago," Nelson said. He lifted his chin, and Sally squeezed his hand.

I stood wobbling on my feet like that drunk driver, like a poacher, a villain, a reprobate. I felt unclean before them, unworthy to speak another word. All the discomforts of my secret were aroused and threatened to overwhelm me. I didn't want to hear another word. As if it would be me somehow, my name, Reuben Dale, an indictment from their lips. But it was impossible, I knew. The mind condemns the innocent inside us, throws down its grievances at our feet. Guilty, Guilty, Guilty!

"Look there, Reuben," Nelson said pointing. "There's your boy with his own candle. For his mother, he told me. Isn't that something? He said his bus has been delayed because of the weather, and wouldn't you know it, he gets to celebrate her life with all of us here. The fact of the matter is that there are not enough candles in this town for the loved ones lost. Life is like that. Never seen a night like this one. The angels are about. I'm sure of it."

I looked around to the many standing in the snow holding candles like Dickens' carollers, and there he was, sheltering the flame with his hand. He seemed lost. "You were talking to him?" I said. The obvious didn't discourage me.

"You know, he looked like he could use a friend. He stays at the motel up the highway. I didn't trust him in the beginning, but I don't like to see the young ones alone like that."

"He's a sweet boy, really," Sally said.

"He likes that boat of yours, Reuben."

Their gentle persuasion was an offering, I knew, to do something for him, an opportunity for redemption, a pardon for my contrived wrongs. And inwardly I accepted. It was not bravery or charity, it was not my benevolent nature, it was nothing but the guise of my trepidation just then, and yes, what Lori wanted for me.

"Tell him for me will you, Nelson," I said. "I'll take him aboard in the morning. Tell him ten o'clock."

Nelson nodded. He was puzzled. Then he looked over at the kid.

"I'm not feeling all that well," I said. "I need to go home now. Thank you for the candle."

I left them there by the tree, in the snow and the lights, and a thousand voices in the street. All seemed unreal now, like a shaken Christmas globe. I was inside it and they were looking at me, Nelson and Sally Grommet. But it wasn't admiration or enchantment in their eyes. I had no proof of what they thought, what impressions they had of me. But it seemed that I had done something improper. I felt as if I had failed my new friend, let him down. The way I always did.

Captain on the Bridge

ᢒᢞᢙ

THE RAIN CAME. The snow melted from the limbs and lines, and the streets were thick with slush. I was duly splashed coming down toward the marina. A west coast snowfall never lasted. It arrived and vanished in a day. As I crossed Main Street and looked to where the crowds had gathered in what had seemed something from a child's fable, there were only ruined ruts in the street and dripping awnings and lacklustre shops. Black umbrellas shielded the scattered few hurrying through the rain. I tried to recall the falling snow and the lights brilliant against the night. But there was only Nelson and Sally cradling a tragedy, the kid with his candle, and what I had agreed to do.

When I walked into the marina store, there was someone at the counter with Nelson, a thin fellow making a purchase. He seemed pleased as he turned to me.

"How about that?" he said. "Picking out my Christmas present."

"Great," I said hanging up my hat and coat at the door and wiping my boots. Then I went over to my table and sat down.

Nelson watched me, expressionless. There was a slight nod to his head. He had me worried.

"New depth sounder," the customer said. He wanted to tell me all about it.

Nelson rang it up and handed the man his receipt. "Good for harbours and fog," Nelson said to me.

The man picked up his depth sounder. He looked my way and could see that I didn't care that much. It wasn't that really. I came slowly to the watering hole in the morning. Still the man was undeterred by my lack of enthusiasm and smiled all the way out the door.

"That man's a happy sailor," Nelson said. "Likes all the gadgets. He looks for shipwrecks."

"Shipwrecks?"

"They're up and down the coast. Sailors out when they shouldn't be. Caught in foul weather. Gales and such. Poor decisions mostly."

"I wouldn't go out in bad weather," I said.

"Sally gets them all the time."

I looked at him — Sally in her wheelchair? I must have looked dumb sitting there, confused, trying desperately to connect the dots.

"You know, on the radio," Nelson said graciously. "She has her radio and computer up there and all the weather and sea conditions. Gives the bulletins. Monitors the emergency channel."

How could I not have known? Then I remembered that day when a strong wind nearly pushed us over. June called the Seaside Coastal Station on the VHF radio.

my June — Seaside, over

Seaside — my June, over

Strong wind sudden out of the northwest, Seaside. Tacking windward south of Savary Island. Looking for safe harbour if need be. Update weather, Seaside, over

Gentle breeze in the strait, my June. Moderate by 4:00 PM, over

Reduce sail and return Seaside, over

Seaside confirms, over

Thank you, Seaside. my June, out

"Yes, of course," I said, scrambling so that I didn't seem like too much of a fool. "Sally helped us with a bit of weather in the summer."

"I'll get your coffee, Reuben."

Sometimes a man just feels stupid. He doesn't mean to be. He has no rude intention with his neglect to listen or pay attention. He goes along his merry way and only sees the limited things of his own interest and concern. I had that sinking feeling that I had insulted Nelson by my indifference to Sally. I was nervous waiting for my coffee. Nelson meant that much to me now.

He put my coffee down. Another whale blowing up the rim.

"You're worrying, Reuben," Nelson said.

"It shows?"

"If I lost Sally, I'd be sitting at that blue table myself wondering what the point of all this was. I wouldn't be of much use for a while. I guarantee it. That kid, he'll be gone tomorrow, Reuben. You don't need to do anything if you don't want to. And don't you worry about me."

Nelson had those fine lines in the corner of his eyes that come with age. They radiated like beams from the sun. They weren't laugh lines. He wasn't a laughing fool, not the kind of man who would slap you on the back or bother you with mindless blather. And he wasn't an overly serious man with dry and humourless theories. He had a quality of humility and innocence that was quietly hilarious and irresistible. You wanted to be near him. It was nothing he did. It was who he was. Perhaps it was the loss of Emily that made him so. As if there was nothing left that could defeat him.

I sat with my coffee as he stood behind the counter. How he left it up to me. And my dread bled out through the floor into the sea. The rain stopped and the sun reaffirmed the world among the masts and boats. Then the question.

"I've been meaning to ask you something, Nelson."

"Fire away, Reuben," he said.

"How does one go back to sea after being away from it?"

"You forget how to sail, Reuben?"

"Well, you see, it was June who was the sailor."

"You're not sure of yourself."

"More than that."

"There's not a man who goes out to sea that doesn't know how to pray. Some just aren't cut out to trust like that."

"Like what?"

"That you'll come back."

"Yes, that part."

"One thing I know, Reuben, is that you know you're alive when you're out there with the breezes. Just the ocean and the wind. Nothing else. And if a whale chooses you that one day and you look into its eye, and if you died just then, it just might be the happiest way to go. Just sayin', Reuben. Most people up at the cemetery died in the hospital. Out there is where we all come from. I think that's why we look at it all the time. I see you doing that very same thing. Looking out over the sea. We just can't help it. I trust things like that."

The telephone rang behind the counter and Nelson answered it. I turned away and looked out the window, the snow all but gone along the dock. It was getting close to ten o'clock.

"It's just Sally," Nelson said. "She needs a hand with something. Good luck with the boy there."

"Thanks," I said. Thanking him for so many things.

Then he leaned over the counter. "And don't forget what Starbuck said, *I will have no man in my boat who is not afraid of a whale.* Of course that was olden times. We don't fear them now. They're smarter than the brains that think it'd be all right to push oil out on tankers along this coast. But you get my meaning."

I finished my coffee. It was time. As I stood to leave I noticed one of the photographs on the wall. A little girl with her father. On a beach somewhere. She was holding a pail, thrilled it seemed to be out among the barnacles and crabs. The father, lanky and shirtless, wanted nothing else but to discover life again for the first time. And Sally, I surmised before the accident, took the picture, her shadow cast from long legs. They were a family. I couldn't help imagining their unthinkable future. I felt such sympathy for Nelson and Sally just then. But how easily I abandoned my moment of humanity when I saw Jonas walking down the dock toward *my June*.

When he reached the end of the dock, he stood there with his hands in his pockets, looking down into the boat as if to claim it. Oh, I felt resentment: his secret ways, how he had spoken to me. But I would do it, give him a quick tour of the sailboat, let him touch the wheel perhaps, satisfy his fantasies for the open sea. That would be enough. June would be proud of my contribution to the boy, and Nelson and Sally would be certain of my good character. Then I could return to the simplicity of a good book. And after the satisfaction of words and worlds, I would walk the empty winter streets that would lead me down to my table over the tides. That was something I could manage now.

He turned to me as I came up to him. "Hey," he said.

"Everything is pretty wet," I said. "Step over the rail and onto that seat. Follow me."

"Are we taking it out?"

"No, this boat needs an experienced crew to sail her. I'm just going to show you around. All right?"

"Yeah, sure."

I could see he was excited. His voice though brazen before, was now more like a child's, eager for a cherished toy to be revealed. It was like anyone I suppose, even that man with his depth sounder, or Bert with a new power tool. And I remember holding an old book I had been looking for and thinking how marvellous it was to touch something that had been around for over a hundred years. A story retold over the generations.

Aboard, I unlocked the companionway and motioned to Jonas. I took him down the steps into the cabin and turned on the cabin lights. The interior smelled musty so I left the companionway open to air it out. I looked around. Everything had been put away. It was a neat little cabin, but it was cold.

"I need to turn on the engine to get some heat down here," I said.

Jonas nodded. He was taking it all in from where he stood, the centre of the universe when the sailing day was done. But strange, I did not think of June just then, so distracted I was by him, his presence, my wanting it to end soon. Memories could not be coaxed out of me with him there. To me it was purely a utilitarian meeting, an appointment for a guided tour that could be concluded with one swivel of his head.

I went on deck to the cockpit, and by the wheel I inserted the key to start the little diesel engine. It was stubborn at first but then found its muffled rhythm. Then I returned to the cabin. Jonas was at the navigation table. He was studying the depth sounder and radio. He had pulled a chart out of the cupboard.

"Do you understand all this?" he asked.

"Mostly," I said.

"I don't know if I could ever figure all this stuff out."

"It's like anything," I said. "You have to study; you also have to want to learn."

He went around the cabin now, touching the teak paneling along the wall, the cupboards, the table and the raised trim on the edge of the galley counter. There seemed to be an interest in what he saw in the cabin, not something of sailing, but an aesthetic that drew his attention. The richness of the wood, the array of instruments, books on navigation, charts with their symbols, their depths and bearings, a sailor's datum with navigational plotters and parallel rulers. He liked it all, I could see, how everything that one would need was there: the layout careful and exacting in comfort and efficiency, the hallmark of the Contessa. He checked out the quarter berths and the berths in the fore cabin and he looked in the head. And I felt just then a mild satisfaction that moved me to sit a moment with him.

"I can make a cup of tea," I said.

"Sure," he said.

"Green tea, all right?"

"Yeah."

So accommodating now, something gratified in him at last. I poured last summer's water into a kettle and set it on a burner on the stove. When the kettle whistled I poured the boiling water over the tea bags and set the cups on the table.

"Thanks," he said.

"It's a good boat," I said. "We restored most of the wood and fittings." *We* I said, as if I belonged to another, someone other than me. How the simplest things could draw you back to something that no longer existed. These reminders that rendered the boat as something inert and fallow, tied bow and stern to the cleats. And how I remembered now, June there at the table with her tea, or busy cooking in the galley. Was it this connection of Jonas and June that made me wonder about him? That boy holding a candle for his mother.

"I like the feel of it below my feet," he said.

"The presence of water."

"One day I will sail," he said.

I watched him with his tea. There was no surliness about his mouth. His eyes moved about the cabin, searching for its secrets. It was the way of the ardent, the student, the keen apprentice. Again some vague impression of how a teacher might feel to see her reward in the eyes of an eager pupil. A purposeful moment with Jonas. I knew nothing really about sailing, but I knew enough for him just then. I was a difference-maker holding the stone that could impart, perhaps, glorious ripples in his life. And June had done that very thing every day at her school. Then he turned to me thoughtfully.

"I'm sorry," he said.

"For what?"

"The way I talked to you last time."

"Well, don't worry about it."

He nodded quietly.

And still I wondered. "So you live in south Vancouver?"

"Yeah, I live with my grandma."

"You have plans?"

"Not really. Get a job, I guess."

"Not going back to school?"

"I would like to. But I just want to see things first."

"Like the sea?"

"The sea. And I want to go back to Sarajevo."

"Sarajevo?"

"To visit my mother's grave."

"What happened to her?" I was intrigued by this and the courage that rose in me to know more.

"She wanted to find my father," Jonas said now in a whispering voice. "He disappeared one day and never came home. My mother was told that he was killed by a sniper. It was during the Siege of Sarajevo. I don't remember him much. After the war we left Sarajevo and came to Canada. I was just five years old. But things were still unfinished." His face went ashen all at once, and his hand holding his cup began to shake, a tremor of memories.

"My mother returned to Sarajevo a few years later," he went on. "She thought it would be safe. But she was murdered. I wanted to know why she had to die. My grandmother told me that the wounds of a country and a people are deep and will not be healed in a lifetime. She did not have an answer. I think my mother asked too many questions of the wrong people. Just me and my grandma now. She worries about me. She gave me some money to come here. She always tells me that I deserve to be happy."

The shocking thing of lives — to think we are the centre of the universe and our hurt and our pain are unlike that of anyone else. This is true perhaps because nothing is ever the same, but it feels as if our suffering is the worst of suffering, our misery the only misery. Our loneliness does not include the possibility that others may share our pain, that what is unifying is the very thing we wish to escape from. I could not find a word to comfort him. There was only the sound of the diesel and the bilge pump now. Shafts of sunlight spilled down the companionway. He wasn't a bad kid. I felt some correction in what I had thought. His unexpected civility. And how strange to feel a remote responsibility for him, an obscure and uncertain duty to his mother. A mother has a power, I knew, that cannot be denied, a power that has taken its eternal place inside us, to guide and soothe, a beacon in the long dark nights where, from the depths of our troubles, we call out to her.

He looked at me as if I might have answers for him, but I didn't.

"I'm leaving on the bus tomorrow," he said.

Requiem for
a Mother

⚬

THE CANCER WAS IN HER bones the doctor had told us. She had been ill for many years, her lungs failing her and a cough that she dismissed so selflessly, to spare us, she had thought, from what she knew. It was the smoking that condemned her, not something that sought her out, but something of her own volition as many with lung cancer know, but will not freely admit until the end. By then it was too late, even with the desperation, the profound will to live. There was no more talk of it. What was done was done, even through the appalling treatment regimen, which stole her last months.

It was July, and there in the Royal Columbian Hospital in New Westminster, we sat in the family lounge outside her room waiting for the nurse. My father sitting grimly could not muster a moment's encouragement for his boys. Walter consoled him while Lyle, with such devastation in his face, sat silently and rigidly, holding on to himself lest he fly apart. He was too wounded to function much longer, waiting for his last moments with her. One by one, the nurse would call us to her room to say goodbye. We sat with our thoughts, the sad agony of our preparation, the realization that we would never see her again, that her life would end, and she the anchor, the heart and soul of our family, would be lifted from our lives.

She always did without. That dutiful act of a mother comes naturally, I suppose, out of a sense of maternal responsibility, a part of her driven to protect and nurture, a gentle ferocity that she so willingly accepted. Not a complaint would escape her lips. Her portion on her dinner plate was always smaller, not to compete with the fare that growing teenagers could pack away. And pie, she would always forego a piece for herself so that the apes of consumption had their good fill. But still there was that satisfaction to have fed, to have looked upon the satiation in the faces of boys becoming men, to have created a feast for her own creations.

My father too, earnest with his food, would shake his head at such swift dispatch of groceries, but he would look down the table and see how pleased she was. And all was well just then. If there was sorrow in her heart, or fatigue weighing down her bones, well, she wouldn't show it.

Walter was first to be called in. I looked up into his broad face as he stood up beside our father, his hand resting on his shoulder so briefly, tenderly. He was so big now; beat all the Dales with his bulk. And that sense he carried, that was not mass but the burden of the eldest. He would be needed now, to fill in the gaps of her leaving, to help our father, to hold him up when his knees would surely sink. One could never know the realities of a loss, the many ways that lives are irrevocably changed. Walter had a young family. Our father would be alone. And I knew that is what she would say to him. *Look after your father, Walter.*

After a time Walter returned. His eyes were deep and red and he fought against the coming tears, but then our father stood to meet him and wrapped his arms around his oldest son. There was no sound, only the sorrowful shaking of Walter's shoulders. Such moments did not seem possible or predictable. They were never planned for, anticipated, never something to be rehearsed so that you would get it right. The spontaneity of love and affection was so simple, honest and real.

Lyle was next. He struggled to his feet, always his bad leg giving him trouble, the mobility of an old man now. Such a sad thing to watch, how he wasted away, so thin and gaunt by his many pain medications, unable to do the heavy work at the garage — no crawling under cars or wrestling tires onto ready rims. He rarely spoke to me, so bitter he was. I never blamed him. It was Walter who compensated for him, made it so that Lyle worked the till, prepared estimates and scheduled appointments. When the Gillnetter Hotel called him and told him *to come get your brother*, he would do just that, lift Lyle from his table of empty beer glasses and bring him home to his apartment. That girl and the life he dreamt of never came his way. To know that a dream will never come, with a nightmare in its place, was so singularly sad for me. To know that I could not fix it. Now a mother who had so unswervingly stayed by him could no longer hold up his world. What would she say? *There will be someone for you, Lyle. I'm sure of it.*

And then I could hear Lyle coming down the hall, the hitch in his steps and the unbearable bawling, and our father rising, turning to catch him in his arms. I stood with Walter. We looked on with our slack arms and broken hearts. It was time for me now.

My father looked at me knowingly, a message in his eyes. That was all there was between us just then, all that could be done. In the profundity of expression, gesture and understanding, words were left to silence, a language mute and articulate in the realm of knowing. As I moved by him, he took my hand in his, so briefly and carefully with his great paw. Then he let go as if passing a baton in some journey that I was too young to comprehend.

The short distance to her room and the light from windows splashed at my feet like crumbs that would take me home. Then her name on a chalk board at the door. I entered her room and there she was, facing the window. In the distance the Fraser River carried waters that would pass by her house in Ladner, perhaps in an hour. In that moment, I wondered what she was thinking. But then I remembered what the doctor said. *The morphine might make her confused.* I approached cautiously. Flowers and cards on a table beside her bed.

"Mom," I said quietly. She turned to me in her greyness, her sleepiness;

the oxygen mask slipped down over chin. Then the slow blinking of her eyes.

"Reuben, sit," she said. She patted a space on her bed.

I sat beside her. I could hear the wheeze and strain of her lungs, her shocking thinness. I took her hand. "Does it hurt?" I asked.

"Oh no, not right now. I'm all right."

What could I say to her? Life so reduced to that essential thing. "I love you, Mom."

"Oh, Reuben."

There was no divine symphony of angels just then, just the two of us. Then she pointed to a card on the table. I took it. *Thinking of you*, it said over a painting of wild flowers in a meadow.

"Read it," she said.

I opened it. Neat handwriting in the blank spaces.

Dear Helen,

What an odd friendship these past few months. You seem the kind of person who could have been a friend for a lifetime. There is so much that a mother must do. And when tragedy comes, well, we don't have all the answers. We can only tend to our children in the best way we can. We have all felt the sorrow. And now you have another challenge. I pray you will find peace. And I hope that what I have to say will bring you and your family some comfort. Donny has been released from prison. I know this might concern you, but he has gone through a remarkable change. He only wishes your forgiveness. It has been my utmost wish that all things be made right. But this cannot be so. We cannot undo the things that happened. We can only forgive if we are able. Perhaps in time. I leave you with my prayers.

Your friend,
Carol Rouse

I put the card back on the table. Such a thoughtful letter to my mother. And that friendship that belonged only to her and Mrs. Rouse was so innocent and remarkable, the qualities and purpose of two women, mothers. "Did everyone read it?" I asked her.

"Yes."

"Lyle?"

"He took it hard. It opened up something inside him. I think he's going to be all right. Yes, I believe so."

"I'm glad."

"Can you forgive yourself, Reuben?"

"I don't know."

"Try."

"I will."

"Forgiveness carries the very meaning of life."

"Yes."

"I'm so wise now."

"You always were."

"I like June. She's good for you. Go have children, Reuben."

Then she closed her eyes. She was asleep. I kissed her cheek and stood a moment. She rested on the edge of her life. Out on the river, tugboats towed log booms, and an endless stream of cars crossed over the arch of the Pattullo Bridge.

She died later that night. Our father was with her. There had been nothing more for her to do. We all came together to make the necessary arrangements, notices, a unifying time in a family. A numbness took care of us, assisted in the difficult decisions and moments, rallied our strengths and saw us through to the service. And how strange to notice humour emerge now and then, with always a reference to our mother as if she were a part of the joke or even a conspirator there in the periphery of her grieving family.

The service was at the Ladner Fisherman's Hall. I helped Walter and Lyle set up rows of folding chairs. It was a hot day and we left the doors open to receive a freshening breeze from the river. "A rightful place," our mother had said earlier. "It is as good a church as any. I won't have words written on a page spoken over my remains. No, something personal would suit me fine. Something plain. Nothing complicated with verses that I never understood. No fuss."

There was a table with tea and sandwiches at the back of the hall for the reception that would follow a brief service. Our mother's sisters sat with our father at the front; they were solemn but attentive. A closed casket lay there before them and a vase of yellow roses from the Chinese grocer on Elliot Street, with a photograph of her taken at Ladner Harbour. The river was in the background as it always seemed to be.

The Dale brothers greeted respectfully the many people who arrived to honour her. How they would touch my arm and tell me some small thing, neighbours, and others who I didn't know. It was no small thing at all, but things that needed remembering, graces released like doves. Lyle was managing, shaking hands and kissing cheeks, a gracious and grieving son. And June sat at the front beside my place, waiting so patiently and reverently. I wanted her to be near me, her presence like a rock that I could hold onto if the seas began to rise. But all was calm that day as if our mother could influence such things, heard my invocation and stilled the anxious fuse that ran through me.

When everyone had entered, Walter and Lyle took their seats. I sat with June. I waited for her hand, the firm certainty of it. And I wondered just then as I often did, why she chose me, what quality I had that made her want to close her hand over mine. Just a passing thought. Then Walter rose and went up to the podium at the front of the hall. He said a few words about our mother, a loving thing that he did for our father. I was so proud of him, his courage. He welcomed others to come up and offer a memory, and many did just that. All was going well. It was simple, just what our mother would have wanted.

Then at the end of the ceremony, so it seemed, our father suddenly and without having told us earlier, stood up from his chair and walked to the podium. Walter stepped aside and watched with such blank wonder, uncertain what our father, Archie Dale, was about to say. I knew that it was not part of the program.

His big hands dropped onto the podium like hams and he stood and faced the mourners. Then he put his hands in his suit pockets and pulled out nothing. Still he stood there. I thought that perhaps he had left something he had written at home. I was feeling badly for him. People were looking at one another, feeling the same unease. Walter was about to take him by the arm before he embarrassed himself completely. It seemed that he just couldn't do it, couldn't say what he wanted to say. But he wasn't up there to say anything at all. He was up there to sing. And he did.

"Summer Wind," a nostalgic song of love, a melody from a time in their lives. With all his fears, he mustered enough courage to sing that song for her. An intimacy I had never imagined, sharing a part of himself that he saved for her. Though he was no Frank Sinatra, his delivery and key were perfect and his voice full and rich. The tears in the hall never had a chance, uncontained on every cheek. How strange it was to realize on the day of her service, how much he loved her. It was also a fitting farewell for him, as it turned out. He had been sick himself, hiding the illness in his blood for a long time. He would never take anything away from her, turn the attention to himself. Years of pumping gas and breathing benzene vapours would finally kill him that same year on the first day of winter in 1979.

The Invitation

∾

I WAS ON MY WAY to Salty Dog's Used Books the day after I had given Jonas a tour of *my June*. Ever since, I had been thinking about him. The wind and rain pushed me along the sidewalk like a wet hand on my back until the uncertain idea in my mind turned into a plan. It was dark enough out in the street for the Christmas lights in the window to have an effect on me. It put me in a generous mood. As I pushed open the door, a bell rang, and the owner looked up.

"Haven't seen you in a while, Reuben," she said from a stool behind the counter as I stood at the door wiping my feet.

"Yes, it has been awhile," I said. She was a large blond-haired woman wrapped in a purple shawl and layers of coloured silk scarves. She wore large looping earrings made of abalone that nearly touched her shoulders. She did psychic readings in the evenings. Since I couldn't remember her name, I had no idea how she could have remembered mine. It seemed that with some people names stick right away. It takes me about three times before I get a name right. Nelson Grommet would be the exception. I suppose with Nelson, it was easier because I just found him such a fascinating and likable man. But with her, I knew it was an unusual name, not something I would remember even after three times. And if I guessed, well, that might be a huge embarrassment. Then likely she would forget my name the next time I came in. I wasn't used to being the recipient of greetings from shop owners. June would spend most of her time chatting at the till while I bypassed the cordials and went right to the books or whatever it was.

"So what are you looking for this time?"

A dubious tone there. She made it sound as if I were in there all the time, as if the store were my personal library. I suppose she might have been a little sore because she never had the books that I had been looking for. Her name started with an M. "Sailing," I said walking up to the counter and searching down the rows of bookcases.

"What about sailing?"

"How to . . ."

"Everything about sailing is down at the end there," she said. "There's a wall of books on how to sail. There's been more than a few Seaside sailors from the last thirty years who have had their time on the water, and then one day just decided to pack it in. Had no more use for their manuals and handbooks. I suppose they were too old or too dead."

Her laugh was a little insensitive, I thought. Her name sounded like moor or mirror but longer. It was on her business card. There was a stack of them on the counter in a clam shell designed for such things. I could feel my eyes lowering, discreetly you know, trying to read one of them. But then I thought that she might be thinking that I was looking down at her breasts — such an indiscretion now. Oh, I did notice the bare skin of her enormous cleavage and how it heaved out into space. That was the second thing to greet customers when they came into her store, and I would be lying if I said that I hadn't marvelled at how her deep inhalations inflated them. My God, I thought, suddenly catching myself. Did I just sexualize her without really knowing it? Perhaps I was influenced by some primal male reaction to the very thing that sustained us, the nurturing embodiment of a mother. I needed to move away from her, lest my eyes deceive me and leapt upon them. But I had another question.

"Do you happen to know when the bus comes?"

"To Vancouver?"

"That's the one."

"Noon," she said. "It's usually on time."

I thanked her for the information and browsed my way down the book aisle. It was a fine store with original wooden floors that sawed and squeaked under your feet. The bookcases were of cedar with their rich aromas that mingled with the musty nostalgic smell of aging books. There were chairs here and there if you wanted to sit a moment, a good place to be when I had a mind for such pleasures. It didn't appeal to me much now, but since the bus would arrive in an hour, I had plenty of time to feel my away around books filled with a thousand sleeping dreams, their embossed spines in easy reach like pet store puppies hoping to be picked. And there was something else that I had a mind for, an idea shaping in my head. I would talk to her about it. Her name ended . . . with something sounding like eel. I was getting closer.

I selected three books: *West Coast Sailing, The Sailing Handbook, Charting the Salish Sea.* The latter was a newer book, a glossy dust jacket of spinnakers and tilting decks. I brought them up to the front to pay for them. She was talking on the telephone, making her appointments for her evening readings. Her eyes were distracted, looking to the street through the window. I made my move and picked up a business card from the counter. No breasts in my way this time. I had the card in my hand, and there it was, PSYCHIC READINGS BY MUIRGHEAL. Yes, I remembered now. I had done it. Her name sounded like more-iel. I was in fine shape now.

She hung up the telephone. "I see that you have found a few," she said to me.

"Yes, just what I was looking for."

She looked at the prices on the inside of each book and entered them in the cash register. "That'll be twenty-four dollars," she said.

I pulled out my wallet and thumbed out a twenty and a ten-dollar bill and handed them to her.

"No one pays with cash anymore," she commented, handing me my change and a few bookmarks.

It was then I chanced my pitch. "So, I didn't find the book that I have been looking for."

That look of hers. "What one?" she asked as she handed me a bag with the books.

"*Moby Dick*," I said.

"No, no *Moby Dick*."

"You see, I have a paperback, a 1961 Signet Classic, but I like to collect the old cloth-bound books, first, second or limited editions."

"I remember."

I hung in there. "I was wondering, Muirgheal," I said, "if you have any way of finding me a copy."

"I don't think you could afford it."

"I can pay."

"I heard that a first edition was going for $50,000. You want to pay that much, Reuben?"

"No. Maybe, just see what you can do, something more reasonable."

"Well, I have a few contacts. I network with a few used bookstores around the country and in the States. A Facebook group, you know. We discuss rare books and such."

"Could you see if you can find one for me? I would settle for good condition."

She picked up a pen and wrote on a piece of paper. "Herman Melville's *Moby Dick*, cloth-bound, good condition."

"Thanks," I said. I gave her my telephone number and a most heart-felt smile. I won her, I could see — a sweet smile for a moment's kind-ness, with my eyes looking into hers, pretty eyes really, blue. Perhaps a bit too deeply as I noticed the slight tilting of her head. What was that? Then it occurred to me, she was a psychic. She may have known exactly what I had been looking at, what I was up to. I wanted one last look. Oh, it was horrifying, the strain that it caused in me. It wasn't the arousal that distressed me. It was the fact that it was there at all so soon after June died. I had to stop thinking. I had to get out of there.

The bus station was a block up from Main Street. The rain had let up, but there was a shoving wind that was raw, and it found its way down my neck. The winter banners flapping in their brackets and pyramids of dirty snow book-ended the intersections. I moved up the sidewalk, humped over with my coat done up so tight that it was choking me. I always seemed to underestimate the weather. At times the sea would flash all at once as if the sun were about to break through. I would set out with a light coat anticipating a pleasant walk, but then I would get caught in some deluge that flung down on me from the mountains. I had always thought that the weather comes from the sea. It was like reading the morning papers, a look out across the strait, some rational interpretation, and then it would come, rain or shine. Now it seemed that on any given day a warm breeze would turn into a gust that would take your hat. But I must say that it kept me alive, kept me in the game, to feel the world that way. And now there was something for me to do, something that I had thought of on my own, something that I had decided.

Jonas was standing under a shelter in front of the bus station. He had a packsack slung over his shoulder. He turned to see me coming up the sidewalk, watching some old guy struggling against the wind, a bag billowing in his hand. He continued watching me as I came right up to him. He didn't have a clue why I would be there, what I wanted from him. He just stood and looked at me, flat, strange, as if he had forgotten who I was.

I handed him the bag. He took it and looked inside. "What's this?" he said.

"A few books."

He removed one and thumbed through it. Then he did the same with the others. "Thanks," he said, still with a confused look. He wasn't expecting anything like that.

"Come back in the spring."

"Are you serious?"

"I'll take you out."

"Why?"

"Just read the books. Then we'll take it slow out there. You might be a natural sailor."

"Why are you doing this?" he insisted.

"You need a hand, that's all." I removed a bookmark from my pocket and wrote down my telephone number. "Here, call me."

He thought about that for a moment as the bus turned up the hill from Main Street. Then he nodded. He understood now it seemed. We stood there awkwardly for a few minutes as several passengers stepped off the bus. The driver waited by the door.

"Got to go," he said.

I placed my hand on his shoulder just as he stepped on the bus. I saw how he hesitated and turned to see my hand slide down his arm. Then he kept on going. I wondered what he thought just then. I meant nothing really. It was more a gesture of acknowledgement. Perhaps just to show him that I cared, that I wasn't an "asshole" after all. As the bus pulled away, there was both a sense of satisfaction and apprehension. Fear had always been the victor. But now I had done this thing for Jonas, an invitation I couldn't retract. Nor could I reconcile my fear of sailing and the need to continue June's legacy, to throw out a stone and accept the responsibility of all that would manifest. It would be some glorious and wonderful adventure. Or a tempest I couldn't stop.

Bad Blood

I STOOD BEFORE THE big bookcase in the living room. I still had a few minutes before I had to leave for my doctor's appointment. My blood tests were in. It's a worry when they call *you*. They wouldn't do that unless it was important, something to discuss, something wrong. They could have just told me on the telephone that I had six months to live. No, they wanted me to sweat for a few days, conjure up all manner of ailments and outcomes. My father had bad blood, and it killed him quickly. I looked it up on the internet, symptoms and causes. But I never pumped gas at his garage. Oh, I used self-serve pumps like everyone else. Perhaps inhaled those fumes now and then. I wondered how many times I had filled my gas tank over the years. I had to get my calculator out. One tank a week is 52 times a year multiplied by, say forty years, and that's 2,080 times that I stood there sucking in fumes. It didn't look good.

As I was thinking myself into this depression, my eye caught the spine of a book, and I pulled it from the shelf. Mint condition for a paperback, though a few of the corners were turned up slightly and the pages had taken on that antique yellow bloom. The cover had a painting of Ahab holding a harpoon. It seemed his face had been clawed with a fork and his eyes gouged out. The white whale characterized on his chest spouted blood. A little grim. I opened it, a random page, and how the eye finds it: *Drink ye harpooners! Drink and swear, ye men that man the deathful whaleboat's bow — Death to Moby Dick! God hunt us all, if we do not hunt Moby Dick to his death!*

I put it down on the table beside my reading chair by the living room window. I had a good view out to the street and saw Bert walking his little dog, a Chihuahua with hair shooting out the tops of its ears. I wondered if that was his compromise for the hours he spends in his shop. The redemptive stroll down the street and back, a plastic bag swinging in his free hand to appease the local bylaw. It pained me to see a big man like Bert kneel down like that, then try to get back up again with the bag and a dog on a leash. A little dog like that didn't seem worth it. And the neighbour on the other side of me, Rollie, retired from the RCMP, liked his dogs a little bigger, spaniel size. At times Bert and Rollie would walk their dogs together. They would meet in front of my house and then sniff one another for a good minute, the dogs I mean. It seemed I had too much time on my hands. I hated waiting for appointments.

I walked to the clinic with the sun splitting through the clouds, the air still and cool, with my mind racing headlong toward my fate. I didn't have to wait long before I was led to the examination room. The waiting was excruciating; finally I heard a rattle outside the door. I was a little upset when the doctor walked in staring down at my chart, reading it for the first time, I surmised, flipping the pages with some privileged speed-reading ability. It wasn't Dr. Chu.

He looked up from the chart and stuck out his hand. "Dr. Bender," he said.

Great. "Oh, hi," I said. "I was expecting Dr. Chu." He looked like Doc in *Back to the Future*. I couldn't talk to this doctor; I didn't feel like starting over with him.

"He'll be away for two weeks," he said. "I'm covering his patients until he gets back."

"Maybe I'll just wait."

"Well, Mr. Dale, your blood test shows areas of concern. I don't think it can wait."

I could sense that he knew better because of the way he looked over his reading glasses. Bad news is bad news. I wanted to get it over with. "So, what is it?"

"So let's have a look," he said. He sat down on the bench beside me. "I'm a little worried about your blood sugar. I think you have Type II Diabetes."

"Really?"

"Yes, not unusual for a man your age."

"Okay." What about the leukemia?

"Your cholesterol is high. There is a risk of complications. Coronary issues. Stroke implications."

"Lovely."

"I see also from Dr. Chu's notes that there is high blood pressure on board."

"All that from a blood test."

"We can manage it, you know. Don't be too concerned."

"So my father died of leukemia. Nothing like that in my blood?"

"No, blood counts seem fine."

"What do I do?"

"I'll write you some prescriptions. They will assist you in managing your blood sugar, cholesterol and blood pressure. And something that will thin your blood. As we age, the arteries can become restricted. The pharmacist will put the medication in a package for your convenience. It is called a compliance pack. It tells you when to take your medicine. It's a daily medication log so that you can keep track. Very simple. Have you had this before?"

"No, it's all new to me. I take the tranquilizers. I'm okay with that. I only need them sometimes."

"Are they working well for you?"

"They help take the edge off."

"I can increase the dosage for you, if it isn't enough."

"I'm good for now."

"You might want to talk with Dr. Chu about that." He was scribbling away now.

"About what?"

"Dosage. It's not uncommon, you know, as our anxieties increase as we get older, to modulate the dosage."

"I feel pretty good, you know."

"We often don't know the trouble until it's too late."

Now that scared me. "I walk. I've lost weight. How bad can it be?"

"Mr. Dale, as we age, medicines can provide us relief from many health issues. Not to worry. These are quite safe and effective. The side effects are of a minor nature."

"Like what?"

"With some of them you might feel a little tired. A stomach upset. Nothing to be concerned about."

"I like to know these things."

"Mr. Dale, I appreciate your concern. Take these to the pharmacy. They are for your own good."

I was becoming angry now. It started in my stomach and then began to come out of my mouth. "I think you're going a little too fast here, Dr. Bender. I really do. I need to think about this."

"Mr. Dale, I believe that you are underestimating your condition. The reports suggest that your health could be compromised without immediate intervention."

There was scolding in his voice. *Trust me.* I took the handful of prescriptions and stuffed them in my coat pocket. I was relieved that I didn't have leukemia — all that worry. But there was something that didn't feel quite right, and it wasn't a condition or a malady. There was something about him. He left the room before I had my coat zipped. He didn't like my questions, and I didn't like his answers.

Back at the drugstore it seemed like the same crowd was waiting. I wasn't feeling good about my doctor's appointment. He made me feel like a moron. I felt as if I had just surrendered to him the rights over my body. When it was my turn, I spoke to the pharmacy technician. "Can I get a copy of the side effects on these prescriptions? I just want to give them a read before you fill them. You know, to make sure I can tolerate them."

"Absolutely," she said cheerfully.

She took the prescriptions and wrote down the name of the drugs.

Before long, she called me over and gave me several sheets of paper on pharmacy letterhead. She pointed to one of the sheets.

"See here," she said, "these are the interactions and possible side effects. A page for each medication. Have a look at them, and I'll be happy to answer any questions that you might have."

"Thanks," I said. She was a nice girl. "Do you always have a line-up for prescriptions?" I asked her curiously.

"Yes, it's always pretty steady."

I thanked her again, took the handouts and prescriptions, and left. I had to get to a neutral location, somewhere to have a cup of coffee so I could read all the information. And I needed to calm down. The more I thought about my visit with Dr. Bender, the angrier I became. I didn't believe that Dr. Chu would have written me any prescriptions without talking about alternatives. It was a good excuse to go down to the marina. Nelson might have some insights. But I wouldn't bring it up directly in case he was using such medications himself. And Sally, too, could have an issue that needed medication. I wasn't that stupid or naïve. I suppose it was just Dr. Bender's manner that got me riled. And that surprised me once again, the anger I thought I never had.

All that walking seemed pointless somehow, negated by a doctor's assertions. I felt unwell all at once, stricken with the infirmities of my age. But how could that be? I didn't feel sick. Oh, I could see the flushing in my cheeks, and I was a little tired in the afternoon, that was true enough. And June, well, she was fit and trim but died of a sudden stroke. Then again, the doctors told me she had something that had always been there, a weakness in a blood vessel in her brain. It was only a matter of time.

Nelson was decorating a Christmas tree when I walked in. I hung up my coat and hat. "Is that a real tree?" I asked him.

"Sure it's a real tree."

"I like the smell of a real tree." I said.

"Sally takes the needles and stuffs them in cushions."

"Good idea," I said.

"Let me turn on the lights here, Reuben, and I'll get your coffee."

"No hurry. I've got some reading to do."

"Doesn't look like a book you got there."

"No, just some research." I sat down at my table and placed the medication handouts in front of me, stacked neatly. I pulled out my reading glasses.

Nelson turned on the Christmas lights. It was a fine place to be just then with the lights and the stove and the sea out the window. He was watching me. I knew he was curious.

"So what is it you're researching there, Reuben?" he asked as he walked over to my table.

I looked up at him, my friend and confidant now. And then I had this feeling, a sense not to risk some poorly timed comment. I didn't want to start anything that I would regret. I had a mind to put the handouts back in my pocket and just enjoy my coffee. But he saw them there plain enough. There was the slight squint of his eyes and then that Nelson Grommet rumination that was already deliberating, ready it seemed to deliver an impression, or perhaps an opinion. But before I could answer he just turned away. Nelson had that rare quality of discretion, an ability to know what to say and when to say it, or perhaps to say nothing at all.

I looked at the first handout, read the warnings, the side effects: *muscle problems, liver problems, swelling of face and lips and tongue, vomiting, fatigue, yellowing of the eyes and stomach pain.* Then I read another sheet, then another, and then the last one: *headache, diarrhoea, bruising, nose bleeds, itchy skin and life-threatening bleeding.* I looked at them again, trying to understand, trying to comprehend how these drugs would be helpful, how they could save my life. My God, I thought, the swelling of ankles and feet, nausea, fainting, a pounding heart beat, deadly bleeding. The list seemed like a nightmare of possibilities, complications, a host of effects that seemed outrageous and injurious, effects that seemed to eclipse the very condition that it was designed for. Some irony of medicine, it seemed to me, to counsel a patient to turn down a road of uncertain ends, a road of indisposition, to ward off illness. But it was not so simple, I knew.

When Nelson returned, he had two cups in his hand, which he set on the table and sat down with me. "Everything all right there, Reuben?" he said.

"I don't know. The doctor doesn't think so."

"I know those sheets," he said.

I picked up my coffee cup. The sperm whale trembled in my hand. I put it back down. "You can't even eat a grapefruit with some of this stuff," I said. I was a little down now.

"Your doctor wants you to take them."

"Yes, but he's not my doctor. He's filling in."

"Dr. Bender?"

"That's him."

"You see that boat out there, Reuben, the one that draws your eye, the one that you could never imagine owning?"

"It's hard not to notice."

"That yacht there belongs to Dr. Bender. And he didn't buy it with his wages. I'm just sayin', Reuben, sometimes it seems that he recruits, starts the older folks down a path with their medicine. I'm not saying that all medicine is bad. No, but there's money in it for the doctors. They won't tell you right out. Dr. Bender had a practice in Vancouver before he settled in Seaside. Some drug company back east had him on a lecture circuit for a while. Published papers. Slick marketing, you know. And everyone goes along because they trust their doctors."

"How do you know all this?"

"A few years back there was a fella' that worked for me. He was retired and liked to be around boats. I hired him for the summer to do the odd jobs around the place. Everyone called him Dobber. He had a bit of a condition and was on blood thinners. He just started on them. Well, one day in the heat Dobber fell sick, and we had to take him to the hospital. He didn't get past emergency before he bled to death. Didn't lose a drop of blood. He bled out on the inside — in his brain. Dobber's family thought it was his medication that did it. Of course there were no takers on that one. They sought legal counsel and found out some interesting things, but they didn't get far. They ran into a pretty big machine and had to drop any action. They didn't have the money."

"My God!"

"I'm just sayin', Reuben, there's always something else a person can do. I'm not telling you that you shouldn't take them. That would be foolish. I'm going to be seventy-five next summer and I'm not on a single thing. Take my salmon oil and vitamin D, watch my diet. No cheese, and cut back on red meat. Healthy snacks for my blood sugar. And I go up to Thunderbird Lookout when I can. A good hike. Gets the heart rate up. I know that you like to walk. You might want to try that one; it's just east of town. You'll love the wrens and thrushes in the woods."

I liked my odds listening to Nelson Grommet. I felt better. I turned the handouts face down. "I never leave here empty handed," I told him.

"Well, if you live long enough you learn a thing or two."

I laughed. "So that kid's coming back in the spring. I'm going to teach him how to sail." My confidence swelling as I sat with Nelson.

"It's never a wrong thing to do something because you want to. You see, you have no one to blame then."

"June helped him," I said. "I think I can too. She would like that."

Nelson only nodded. He didn't offer what I thought he would offer. There was no acclaim or praise. And that made me feel doubtful some-how. I wanted his approval. I wanted to see it in his eyes. But he only sipped his coffee and turned to the sea.

Trail of Lost Dreams

※

I BEGAN TO WONDER if I was spending too much time down at the marina. At times I felt as if I had said something wrong. Nelson would look away. An expression that I fully expected to see was absent and something else in its place that I didn't understand. Oh, he was still Nelson, a man that I admired. I felt I should go to Thunderbird Lookout, as he had suggested, some other place to wonder what had happened between us. I needed to clear my head. I had this anxious quality that interfered with my own discernment, reading too much into things, worried too much what people thought of me. What did it matter? People flocked to June, her energy, and so there had always been a portion of interest in me. I went along for the ride, and it was enough. Now flying on my own, there was only me, my words, the essential Reuben Dale. Who was he really? It was unsettling to feel the loss of a leg like Ahab, half a man pitching headlong and mad into the future. I could sense June, her presence like a phantom limb, but she was nowhere to be found.

I drove east of town along the winding highway. There was frost on the rural lawns, and fence posts bristled with a fine white fur. All clear skies and the sun as low as it would get for another year — the solstice and the tug of all things lost inside me. The trail wasn't far now, past the last house and through a forest with the ocean bright beyond the trees. I parked in a clearing made for hikers above a stream, Thunderbird Creek that spilled its charging, chilled waters into the sea. There was a sign with a map of the trail up to the lookout, which said that the trail was moderate, to allow an hour for the return trip. It seemed a simple hike, perhaps steep, but within my abilities. I was a walker and I had the legs for such a trail. I had packed a lunch of peanut-butter sandwiches, an orange and a bottle of water. I had a good polar fleece jacket and my Tilley hat. I was all set. Slipping my arms through my packsack straps, I set off up the trail.

The trail began at a good grade through hemlock and fir. It followed the creek, the hushed roar of it ever present as it tumbled white-foamed and furious over boulders the size of Smart cars. The sun fell across the trail, shards of it filtering down through the high still crowns. Great stumps reared up from the understory of salal and moss-humped rocks. Soon the trail bored deep into the forest, twisting around rock outcrops and crossing small ancillary streams. I could feel a subtleness of unease, which I could not explain. When the trail veered away from the creek and its roar became more distant, I began to experience a remote sense of myself. I felt alone without it as if it had a language that was meant to comfort me. The forest was darker now, away from the light of the creek that was like an illumined scar. Oh, I could still see where the sun found its way to the earth, broken and strewn over ferns and fallen trees. The eyes seek the light, but mostly it was shadow among the thick trunks of ancient trees. Dimness overwhelmed the woods like something spilled. I moved steadily upward, hearing now a new sound.

I stopped to listen. A bird far away and near, the trill of its high, clear song like the tinkling of bells, rapid, ascending. I could not tell where it came from. There was only the sunless expanse of density. It had to be the winter wren that Nelson had told me about. All was silent again.

And then another sound, as if the muted forest was its cue. It was not a song like that of the wren but a lament, a thrush's secret quavering, long and eerie. It emerged from the forested space without a body, inviolable, mystical, as if the song was all that existed. It had a haunting quality that seemed to enter me, touch my sadness somehow. I needed to move. I could feel a sinking inside me.

The trail grew steep, switch-backing up through the trees, then twisting back toward the creek. I could hear it now and the brightening there. I hurried to see it, to feel the sun against my skin. There was an aching in my legs; I was going too fast. I rested for a minute, peering down through the branches to catch a glimpse of water. But the forest's tangled margins were too thick. As I went on, the trail turned away, as if to deceive me, a punishing deviation. I found myself back in the forest with its mood and the thrush's dismal song rasping from its unseen throat.

It was then that I knew I couldn't go on to the lookout. I needed to get down, out of the loneliness of the trees, out of the melancholy of shrouded bird song. I stood looking back down through the forest with anxiety rising in me, something I had experienced before, but then there had always been the safety of June, of home and something to hold on to. But here, with desolation surrounding me, I felt abandoned by the world. I could see a section of the trail far below me. There seemed to be a quick way down through the ferns and soft broken logs. I didn't notice my hunger or understand the consequence of a meagre breakfast of coffee. There was only the returning to the light. It seemed to me that my safety waited there, the familiar sight of my car, and below it the sea spreading out across the strait.

I scrambled down the slope like a fugitive fleeing from an unknown crime, stumbling, sliding on my backside, moving too fast, my hands clutching at branches, the panic in my chest. There was only down. I didn't know why I was even there at all. The forest was an unknowable thing to me, reaching up from the ocean with secrets that were never offered to me. I had been a rural boy, where hedgerows between potato farms, with ducks and muskrats in ditches, had seemed a wilderness.

Then what my eyes had seen was gone. The trail was no longer there, snatched from me like some cruel joke. I was breathing hard, not so much by the exertion of coming down the mountain, but by the shocking realization of being lost, confused, the savage desertion of all that I knew. All about me the curtains of an alien world were drawing closed. I sat down on a log, cold and shivering, and opened my pack — some unconscious deciding now. The peanut-butter sandwiches. I watched all this somehow, detached from the old man on a log, filthy with his adventures, having his lunch. He ate and he rested. Soon I re-entered him and he got up to find the place of his coming, where the trail was obscured by a tree fallen from an autumn storm.

I walked out onto the trail, standing with amazement and fear at my disintegration. Then I followed the trail back down, slow, unhurried, and thankful to hear the rush of the creek and to see my car in the parking lot. Finally I could see the ocean through the trees. I followed the trail down to the beach, emerging into the sun like something born out of the darkness, heaved out like Jonah. All about me was the life of familiarity, the gulls and crows in an expanse of seamless shimmering. The creek flattened over the rocky shore, a muted gurgle now. I dropped my pack by a beached log and continued down over barnacled stones to the very edge of the sea. Cupping my hands, I received the cold brine of it coming in on gentle waves, and I washed the forest from my hands.

I returned to the log and sat down. I wouldn't say that it was peace that I felt or a sense of well-being, for these never seemed possible for me. I always settled for the reasonable tones of order and uniformity. Moods always brighten in the sun. A harbour seal watched me, curious about an unmoving terrestrial thing. One minute its slick rubber head surfaced and then it was gone. Rafts of sea ducks stretched beyond the kelp beds. There was a bald eagle perched on a fir snag down the beach a ways. Boats were out on the water and a floatplane droned overhead. Across the strait, I could see the vague impression of Parksville and Mount Arrowsmith's white nape. Not the same view from the lookout that I imagined Nelson would ask me about. It felt as if I had failed to do the most basic thing, something I had taken pride in, my walking. Just another walk, you know, through the borough of wrens and thrushes. But the abject isolation of the sombre altitudes was more than my sensibilities could bear.

Sitting there, I wondered again why Nelson had not responded to my decision to take Jonas sailing. Why had he seemed so diffident? When the boy first arrived, Nelson had been suspicious of him, and then at the Christmas festival, it seemed he had wanted me to sympathize with Jonas. But when I had come out with the offer to take the boy sailing, Nelson had turned away from me. Had he somehow discovered my past? Perhaps Sally felt it the way a mother can who has suffered so. She would know such things, could look into my face, read the guilt scripted there, etched into cheek and jowl. Or did Nelson doubt that I could sail on my own, teach a young man the ways of a sea I did not understand myself? Perhaps he knew my capabilities, my limitations, a sailor tied fore and aft to the dock. He could see the folly of my enterprise. I had been busy waiting for the sound of applause. And when I took my bow, there had been only silence.

The Grief Group

⁓

IT CAME OVER ME SITTING there looking out at the rain and the dismal street that the Christmas season was supposed to be happy. It was never meant to be celebrated alone, but alone I was. The girls were off living their lives: Lori with her boyfriend's family, and Mandy, well, she was always busy with friends it seemed. I was worried about her, how she avoided me. Perhaps she was angry at life, the quieter of the two, taking the loss of her mother the hardest. Whatever that means. She just didn't want to talk. And I didn't want to talk much myself. The weight of June's absence now so acute that I couldn't bear for Nelson to see me so pathetic, crippled with my sadness, shuffling about with a body of chain mail. So I stayed home. The thought of a walk couldn't move me from my chair, nor could *Moby Dick* intrigue me enough just then to visit old Nantucket. When gravity holds you to the earth, all you can do is stare through the rain-streaked window. It was as if I were waiting for something to arrive, a parcel, a gift, a miracle. Yes, I would have welcomed divine intervention. Even Bert and Rollie were indoors. But there was life in their homes, and cars arriving. I had watched them unload, children and grandchildren, armfuls of colourful presents. And then a knock on their doors, yapping dogs and the sounds of joy.

There was a grief group meeting that evening. I suppose I was mulling it over. The idea of attending scared the hell out of me. Truth be told, I had this absurd notion that something might come along if I just sat long enough. But the day wore on and the light outside began to fade, and I had done nothing but fret. I needed something. The white pills were idle in my pocket. I sensed that there was no peace in them, not even up on the trail. I wasn't going to give that son-of-a-bitch Dr. Bender the satisfaction of upping my dosage. In fact, I wouldn't take the little bastards anymore. Oh, miserable me. The meeting was at seven o'clock.

I sat in my car outside the Seaside Senior's Centre. I wanted to see who went inside, the size of the group. Perhaps I could sit at the back if it was a large group, make myself invisible, and maybe learn a thing or two. What was it that I wanted? I really didn't know. But still I found myself there, curious, anxious. There seemed to be a lot of people going in. Perhaps it was like a lecture. That would be better. No one would ask me a thing, and I would be safe.

I went in and stood in what seemed to be the lobby. There was a chalkboard sign: *Grief Group* and *Knitting Club*. Now that's a problem, I thought. Were they in the same room? I wandered down a hallway. I would just look, commit myself to nothing. I stuck my head in a door. At first I thought that it had to be the wrong room. It was tiny, the size of my kitchen. Six women sat uncomfortably in a circle, and not a ball of yarn among them. "Grief Group?" I managed to croak out. I avoided eye contact, a kind of throwing it out there before I turned away.

"Yes," the answer came, "please join us."

I glanced to the voice, to the shape of a face I knew, the body now in full view, her gaping chest like a shelf. It was Muirgheal from the used bookstore. She was a psychic. Perhaps she never heard me. "This is the Grief Group?" I asked again.

"Yes, this is the Grief Group," she reiterated with that same restrained smile of annoyance. "Please sit," she said pretending not to know me. She wore a name tag. They all wore name tags. It seemed Muirgheal was the facilitator of the group.

I noticed three empty chairs. They were together. I sat down on the one in the middle, my sole refuge, I decided. It didn't last. I wanted to flee in the worst way, my regret flooding in, a rush of fear like a hot wind. But Muirgheal sat across from me, her smile making me keep sitting. This deeply aggrieved me, placed me back in that unlikely position, as if our day in the bookstore together had not been resolved in her, in me. I had been a little preoccupied with her breasts that day. And life knowing this, of course, had tossed me back into the ring of fire. Perhaps it was not grief at all that brought me here but some unconscious longing. Those thoughts wished to exploit me, it seemed, and I could not stop the stream of them. They were the irrational ramblings of a grieving man after all. And there I was among the grieving, to be consoled perhaps, staring down at the floor.

There was quiet chatter among the ladies. "We'll just wait a few more minutes before we start this week's meeting," Muirgheal said. This seemed to settle them.

We sat in our circle in a moment of awkward anticipation. I was the only man. They all seemed so old. But there was one who could have been my age. I was uncomfortable, terrified really. I had this unsettling thought that they were all looking at my balls. I crossed my legs. But my hip soon began to ache and I had to place both feet on the floor. I squeezed my knees together, but that didn't feel good either. A guy has to sit a certain way. He needs the room. Then I held my hands at my crotch but it looked like I was holding them. I was fidgeting with a strange restlessness. I kept my eyes glued to the tile floor, to a stain that looked like Gorbachev's birthmark. I was about to launch an escape, but Muirgheal must have sensed it with her psychic abilities and began the session.

"Now, we have a newcomer with us tonight," she said. She was looking right at me. "Can you tell the group a little bit about yourself?"

"Fuck!" My God, I panicked and had said it out loud. The looks of such stunned consternation. I couldn't speak, couldn't utter another word against the throb of what I knew was my bright pink face.

"Yes," Muirgheal said, "go on."

She handled that well, I thought. I took a deep breath. "My name is Reuben," I began with a seriously dry throat. "We came to Seaside early last summer. You know, to retire." I let it trail off there.

Thankfully Muirgheal left me alone. She wrote my name on a white label with a felt pen and peeled it from its backing and passed it down to me. I stuck it on my chest. Then she turned to the others.

"Tonight we are going to explore how the holidays might affect us," she said. "For some of you this time of year can be extremely difficult. Having the support of family becomes very important. And I realize that everyone does not celebrate Christmas. But still, it can be a depressing time when we are supposed to be so happy. Society has all these pressures. Can anyone add to this?"

The mark on the floor wouldn't let go of me. And I wasn't going to leave it. Muirgheal would have to pry my eyes from it. Then someone began to speak. It was safe, and I looked up. It was Ruby — as her name tag indicated. They proved really helpful. Ruby was tiny in her chair, and she spoke softly.

"I like to bake," Ruby said, "and Stanley loved to eat. Butter tarts, mincemeat tarts, shortbread, and carrot pudding so rich. And fruit cake, the dark kind. That was his favourite. He would gain twenty pounds at Christmas. Yes, he loved my baking. I was always chasing him out of the kitchen. Oh, the smells that would fill our house, goodness gracious. I didn't bake this year. I just don't have the heart anymore."

Ruby was such a sweet lady. There was an immediate heartfelt recognition around the room. We could all relate to her story and the finer details of loss, the intimacy between a man and a woman found in the simple things that we all knew so well. She said it all so lovingly. It didn't seem so hard, to speak of such things.

"We always went south," Bobbi said. She was heavily made up, a certain elitist glitter about her. Perhaps she had a party to go to. "There's a golfing resort near Cabo. That's the place to be. It gets so damn bleak around here that I can barely stand it. I miss the golf. And I miss Gordon too." Then her staccato laugh. "He collapsed on the ninth green. Trust Gordon to choose that. He always shot well on the front nine. Wouldn't you know it, the course marshal wanted us to keep moving."

Doris had a sour look about her. "I don't know that I miss Jim this Christmas," she said. "He never cleaned up after himself. Lord, the trail of his little messes. He never helped with anything, like a dog underfoot. I tried to find him things to do but he just moped about all day. I told him, 'Jim, for Christ's sake, go out and have coffee with that crowd at the Sand Dollar Café, join a group, do something. You can't be sulking around the kitchen all day. It's my damn kitchen, you know!' I'm angry with him, to be honest . . . dying like that. He just gave up instead of making himself useful."

"Thank you, Doris," Muirgheal said. "We'll come back to anger a little later. Any more thoughts about Christmas?"

I was thinking that Muirgheal should contact Jim and bring him back so he could defend himself. That Doris rankled me. I had my own anger now. She knew nothing about what a man needed. I wanted to tell her so, but I managed to keep my mouth shut. I waited for Betty and Shirley to say something. It was their turn. But it seemed they had nothing to offer just then and passed. Perhaps they too, had been put off by the way Doris slammed her husband. Then I remembered something, a small thing that I could share. It calmed me to recall it.

"We did this together," I said. "When Christmas cards came from friends and family, we would open them. But before we would read the sentiment, we would look for the cardinal on the front of the card. It may have been one of those snowy village scenes or country scenes with a farm house, kids on a skating rink, a horse and sleigh with that cheerful and robust family, a Victorian house or just the woods with pine trees or birches or aspens covered in snow. Somewhere there would be a bright red cardinal in a tree, not always, but it seemed like always. And as we admired those cards with our winter bird, June would invite me to shrink down and step into the scene with her. She had a childlike imagination at times. But when the cards came this year, I couldn't open them. I didn't want to look at them on my own. Perhaps one day. Not now."

They all looked at me as if I were the sentimental type, gushing some warm and fuzzy charm. It wasn't me. No, I could never have created such play as June had done, that carefree discovery of imagined worlds. I was no dreamer, not a quixotic bone in my body. I would never do anything I couldn't count on. Now it seemed that my investment in the predictable had left me bankrupt as a pauper.

"Let us talk about anger," Muirgheal said. I was impressed with her composure and gentle diplomacy. "Betty," she said, "can you share any thoughts about anger?"

"I guess I'm mad at Tom," Betty said tentatively. She had a grim mouth and her arms were gathered tight around her as if she were shielding herself against the cold.

"What are you mad about, Betty?" Muirgheal coached.

"Tom had an online gambling debt that I didn't know about," she said. "He kept it from me. We were married for fifty-five years. I thought I knew him, sleeping all those years in the same bed. I'm embarrassed to say I didn't. When he worked at the mill, however, he was better. That kept him busy. He was too tired then to get into trouble."

"Just like children," Doris said. "You have to watch them."

"Gordon never had problems like that," Bobbi said. "Well, he was addicted to golf, I suppose. Where did that get him? But I'm not angry about it. Heavens, no."

"I was never angry at Stanley," Ruby said. "But one day after he died I was a little cross with myself. You see, he had left a whole pie in the fridge. He never had a bite. I hadn't thought to freeze it. It was Stanley's last pie."

"It's not all good memories," Betty said.

"There were times," Doris agreed.

"Stanley was always good to me," Ruby said.

"Don't get me wrong," Doris said, "I wouldn't mind cleaning up after Jim if I could have him back. I don't mean to sound so nasty."

"Tom could tell a good joke," Betty said, "although sometimes it was easy to be angry at him. We were good friends most of the time. You have to take the good with the bad."

"It's the loneliness that makes you angry," Bobbi said. "The things you can't undo. You can't go back."

"Shirley?" Muirgheal said. She hadn't said a word all evening.

"What is grief?" she said in a faded British accent so calm and clear. She looked down at her folded hands, and the room stood still.

"That deep sorrow we feel after loss," Muirgheal said.

"I have no grief," Shirley said. "I have only guilt for its absence."

This was so strange it caused a shudder to go through the group — some quality to her sitting there with her long silver braided hair. She wore a lavender sweater the colour of the twilight sky. It seemed that it took great courage for her to come, to listen to the grieving of others. I understood from what she said that she had nothing to counter the bashing of men. It seemed that they did not see me there. I'll admit a certain resentment with the condescending tones directed at retired men unprepared for a home life. But Shirley had a story to tell, unlike the pettiness of crumbs and idle pitfalls. Such things may well be troublesome for couples that find themselves in constant company, but I could sense a darker sort of disclosure.

"Can you speak more about that, Shirley?" Muirgheal said.

"My husband's name was Dalton," Shirley said with her head tilted down.

"Interesting name," Muirgheal said.

"I thought so . . . at one time."

"Can you talk about him?"

"Well, he was a decent man."

"Yes."

"When he was sober, he had good qualities," Shirley said. Then she slowly raised her head and spoke to Muirgheal now in a determined voice. "A violent man when he took to it. Hard liquor, mostly after work. He worked at a slaughterhouse. Perhaps it was the gruesome work that wore on him. You could smell the gore on his skin. I'll never know. But he got mean after the kids went to bed. Took it out on me. I thought that somehow I deserved it. Can you imagine that? The kids left home as soon as they could. Who could blame them? And when the work was done, and there was a pension for him, his dark storms began to fill a savage emptiness that tormented him. And I was there taking it all. Broke my arm and my jaw. The alcohol was slowly killing him. And I prayed for it, prayed to God to take him. I felt myself dying, too, especially on those nights when I hovered over him with a knife, and I saw in the bedroom mirror my shocking madness. We are all mad by degrees. Finally he did die, and I was glad for it."

"You were relieved?" Muirgheal asked.

"Yes."

"It had to end, Shirley," Ruby said in her tender voice. "It's not a fault to want to protect yourself."

"I'm sorry that happened to you," Bobbi said. Doris and Betty agreed. How such comfort came now.

"You deserve to be happy," I said. It just came out. Then I winced, as it seemed trite all at once, as if happiness was a goal for her.

She turned to me, not a smile at first, but perhaps evaluating me. Was I a safe man? Then she did smile. Perhaps it was a gamble to do so, but I believed it was genuine. She would know of such uncertainties now. I surmised she would never put herself at risk again. "Thank you," she said.

There was nothing ordinary about Shirley. She had a regal head, had known the assassin and met him. Now free, she sheathed herself in what one had to call an effulgent might. The others saw it too.

Muirgheal then looked at me, and I looked at her. She was a different person to me now, a sensibility capable of helping, supporting, cultivating the healing of that small world in Seaside where the patriarchs arrived one by one to their final destination. And how it struck me to be in such company, humbled, grateful for June and a marriage without such woes and tribulations. When the session ended, the anger inside me rested in the shadows like an unknown guest.

Out in the dark of the parking lot I watched Shirley walk to her car. And then she turned all at once and caught me looking her way. I was parked near her. She waited for me, standing outside her car. I was unprepared for what she asked me.

"Do you feel like a bite to eat?" she said.

"Uh, kind of late," I said.

"Oh, just a thought," she said. She unlocked her car and opened the door to get in.

"Where?" I suddenly blurted out, to my utter amazement.

"Athens by the Sea is open late."

"That Greek place."

"If that's all right."

"Sure."

"I'll see you there then."

She drove away and I sat in my car, sat there watching the red tail lights bleeding into the wet pavement, watched her disappear around the corner. I felt sick.

Athens by the Sea

SHE WAS SEATED BY a window. The sea beyond was without shape or dimension. It was only the collar of lights across the strait that gave breadth to it. She was looking out into that black void. A lit candle on the table framed her. How did this happen, I thought, that I would agree to such a thing? Then she turned and saw me standing there. A little wave of her hand and I walked over to the table, struggling with my honesty.

I didn't sit down. "This is awkward," I said. "I shouldn't be here."

"I'm sorry," Shirley said. "I shouldn't be here myself. The truth is that I don't exactly know where I should be."

"I know what that's like," I said.

"I asked you only because I couldn't bear to be alone after that. And the ladies, well I'm not like them. Oh, they're sweet enough. Just company, that's all."

"Maybe a Greek salad," I said.

"Yes, that would be nice. Perhaps a glass of wine."

I sat down at the table. Then a frightful moment as I looked up and met the eyes of a woman I scarcely knew, an acquaintance not an hour old. And the waitress addressed us in that casual way as if we had been doing this forever, a couple sharing the late evening and the soft light of a candle that peeled away a dozen years.

"Please don't take me wrong," she said. "I'm not asking you to have sex with me. It's not that. Well, I liked your story about the Christmas cards and the cardinals. We had them in New Brunswick. I adored them. I thought that you couldn't be a bad man and love cardinals."

That's what honesty looks like, I surmised. The word *sex* like the resounding thud of an axe on my sensibilities; I was certain that June was listening. I wasn't used to such openness. But it wasn't so shocking now really, having listened to her before at the Grief Group. "How long have you been in Seaside?" I asked her. The waitress brought our wine.

"A few months, that's all," she said. "I bought a townhouse in Leeward Court. It's nice, a view over the water. I came by myself. I had to get away. You know, bad memories and all that. And my children, Coreen and Liam, wouldn't you know it; they went away themselves. They are in Africa with one of the NGO's. Africa needs so much help. I'll be going in a month. I miss them dearly. So a fresh start on the West Coast. But it's so hard."

"It's not easy," I said. I looked around the restaurant, the many couples, festive Greek music playing, along with the sprawling ivy on the great potted plants, and the motif from another world that found a home, reinstated there in the blue tiles and artful murals on the stucco walls — a moment at ease with the warm fullness of red wine.

"I don't know if I'll stay," she said. "There's nothing holding me to anything really. You know, like Homer's *Odyssey* — longing for home and all that."

"*I long to reach my home and see the day of my return. It is my never-failing wish.*"

"Now that's impressive," she said.

"I have my moments," I said. "I have that quote on a beer coaster."

Our salads were delivered: glistening peppers and onions, thumbs of feta cheese. I was aware just then, of the pills in my pocket, how I didn't need them, how the wine was loosening me.

"So tell me about your lovely wife."

"June . . . God, I can hardly say her name. Being here is so strange."

"She's not here, Reuben." Her eyes fell on my chest. I was still wearing my name tag. "I think that it's all right to have come. Life goes on."

"Life goes on. But it feels like . . ."

"Like you're betraying her."

"Something like that. Why is that?"

"You don't want to let her go."

"Why would I?" I said with my blood rising, unstoppable now. "I don't get it. *Get over it. Life goes on.* It's not like that for me. I won't betray her. I won't toss her away and forget about her. I don't want to replace her. I won't!"

"I meant no offense."

"Why would you say that? You don't know me. You never knew her."

"You're angry. I'm so sorry."

"This was a mistake." I peeled off my name tag, some unconscious gesture. "I haven't been with another woman. There was only June — my whole life."

And then that moment that I dreaded, when there is an appalling silence and a bruising hurt that stills my wooden tongue. We each turned to the window, to the safety of nothingness beyond the panes.

"It's not a bad thing to talk and share a glass of wine," Shirley said after a moment. There was a measured warmth in her tone, offering a correction between us. "There's no harm in that."

"I guess that I'm just not looking for anything. I'm just trying to get by."

"Why did you come?"

"I don't know. You seemed interesting." Cooling down now, I was aware of that eruption visiting me once again. I could never see it coming. It frightened me. Everything frightened me.

"We're adults."

"My girls would kill me."

"Would they?"

"Maybe not. I don't know."

"I think that when we say that life goes on, we're just hoping that life will be gentle with us, take us to a safe place where we can live our lives."

"Yes."

"I don't have it all figured out, Reuben. I'm treading water. Really."

"I know what you mean." I was so agreeable. I could only offer her my bewildered recognition. Shirley was giving so much of herself, and I was drowning there. That burning in my face. I couldn't find the strength to leave. Relationships were too hard for me. It seemed that I couldn't even sustain my friendship with Nelson. Just talking seemed to me a pointless affair since I had nothing relevant to say, no bites of wisdom or clever anecdotes. Sailing was a lie, walking my only work, my purpose and my virtue. And now that didn't seem enough. I was working my way back to the cave. *Did you hear about the kid who was killed in the snow, run over by a truck, his life over before it began? And his brother Donny Rouse . . .*

"The facilitator tonight . . ."

"Muirgheal," I said.

"Yes, Muirgheal said that the support of family is so important this time of year. And yet I have withdrawn from everything that I have ever known. I couldn't keep my family together. A mother will do anything for her children. But sometimes we are impotent to act when they need us the most."

I nodded. She was going deeper, places that were uncomfortable for me. I took a long drink of wine. There was a fascination now with her language, the gentle probing, like tasting bits of me, as if my answers drew a picture for her. It was odd, but I didn't mind it so much. And somehow she understood my anger, stayed there with me.

"So where are your children?" she asked.

"Toronto," I said.

"Why are you not together?"

"I don't know."

"Sometimes we can't look at the reason. We're not ready to see."

"I think it's me. I can feel myself drifting away from them. Yeah, it's me. I'm letting it happen. June was everything. I don't know what to do. I'm running away from them. Why would I do that?"

"Because you're hurt. A wounded animal retreats to the deep woods to lick his wounds."

"I've been in the woods. It was a frightening place."

"You should have stayed there. Sat down with the bear."

"You're so easy to talk to. How do you know all this?" I asked.

"Would you think I was lying if I told you that I was a psychologist?"

"No."

"The irony stares me down every day. I helped a thousand souls and never a moment's counsel for myself. I was so ashamed that I gave it up."

"I think you're doing pretty well."

"Don't listen to me," she said with a faint smile.

"There's someone else in Seaside who knows a thing or two."

"Who might that be?"

"Nelson Grommet, the proprietor of Seaside Marina. He's a friend of mine. He knows the ways of the sea and all those who dare to know it." A moment of rare insight that I delivered with an uncommon flare, but at once wanted to retract it, comparing her like that.

"Oh, I met him, you know," she said without a hint to my transgression. "I thought at first it was Gordon Pinsent."

"You did?"

"Don't you think?"

"Yes, I suppose. I did actually."

She smiled once again, a good sport. I saw it plain in her face when she looked away after a sip of wine. Her lifted chin revealed wisdom, but there was a loveliness, too, that held her, cupped that good chin and caressed her slightly parted lips. Her eyes that appeared colourless seemed to absorb the room into their dark pondering depths.

"Will you go back to the group?" she asked.

"I don't know. I thought it was all right. But it's sad to see the men dying like that. No one to speak for them."

"You did."

"That wasn't much."

"I won't forget it." She smiled again.

"And you?"

"No, I'll be leaving for Africa soon. I'll be away for three months.

That's a long time to be in Africa. Who knows, I might stay."

"I can't imagine being so far away."

"It's not far when your children are there."

"I guess not," I mused.

"They're all I have now. Loneliness is no companion."

"I know."

"You have a friend at the marina," she pointed out.

"Nelson Grommet."

"Loneliness has no friends," she said, almost Sybil-like.

"What about you?"

"You could be one." She looked at me

"Yes."

"Maybe this was it. A friend for the evening."

"Let's toast to that." I said with a buzzed satisfaction that comes in a glass of wine. We raised and clinked our glasses, and when the bill came, we split it, even to the tip. That seemed fair enough among friends. She would have it no other way. And at the door before we went our separate ways, she put out her hand.

"Shirley Plath-Mellencamp," she said. "Pleased to meet you."

I took her hand, surprised at the firmness in her grip and the celebrity expanse of her name. "Reuben Dale," I said. We shook hands like good friends, and I couldn't help smiling. There was no kiss on the cheek or embrace. We left nothing at the table, just the remnants of our talk. And my anger, well, it would come with me. I was becoming familiar with it, another acquaintance now.

We were friends for that one evening. If it turned out that I would never see Shirley again, then it would have been worth it, one small ripple finding its way home to Athens by the Sea. And I knew, could feel deep within myself, that such ripples could also be rivers, spreading their unpredictable nature beyond my own reckoning of the world.

Dinner with the
Grommets

✍

IT SEEMED SUCH A WASTE, having a glass of wine alone. But I did, grew accustomed to it, and looked forward to the late afternoon when the day was done to uncork the numbing agent of my choice, never the white pills. There was no fun in them, not like a glass of good red with a book, or while watching some inane television program to pass the time. That's what it was really, passing the time, soothing the loneliness with forgetfulness and blurred detachment. The loathsome gall of the world to sentence me to a solitary life.

Now a late January malaise when the days seemed laboured and the brooding mountains crouched down over the town. Even the stout-hearted could feel how winter dragged on. I was stuck there, held fast to a routine of merciless boredom. I had a friend, perhaps two or even three, a shrink, a psychic and sailor, and still I did not seek them out, so conditioned now to my misery. *Loneliness has no friends*, Shirley had said and I must have believed it. There was a great inertia that seized me on those sunless days. Walking had become a redundant business. And the kid was coming with the spring and there were books to study, charts and maps to review, skills to learn and perhaps reaffirm. Get down to the boat, you would think. *But what's this long face about, Mr. Starbuck; wilt thou not chase the white whale?* So when Nelson Grommet called and invited me to dinner, it came like a rope thrown to a man overboard. The pun of which was buoyantly overlooked.

I walked down Mariner Street with a bottle of wine tucked under my arm and the evening sky over the strait teasing with thin fingers of colour. It was the rare hint of a sun that had all but abandoned Seaside. The wind off the dark water was cold and seemed to clutch at my neck. All was wet and slick. The lights along the dock summoned nothing, the boats jostling nervously. I hadn't been down to visit Nelson for over a month, and as I reached the door I felt an apprehension that I thought had left me some time ago. That table with my coffee had been my salvation, his friendship a healing balm. But I remembered how it was the last time I was there, the news I had, and his turning away. It was never reconciled, no explanation for his coolness. It troubled me not to know, to guess and to doubt, and to have stayed away because I couldn't bear his disapproval. And now there I was, an invited guest. The store was closed so I knocked.

Nelson answered right away. "Come in," he said. "I've been waiting by the door. Wouldn't hear the knock from upstairs with the wind and the flapping. Hang your coat here, Reuben. Good to see you, you know. I wondered where you'd been. Sally asked me to call you. Over there by yourself and all."

"Well, it's been a strange time for sure," I said as I hung up my coat. "I brought a bottle of red wine. I hope you like red."

"I won't throw you out," he laughed. "No, just kidding, Reuben. Sally and I are partial to red. I like the colour. Sally likes the taste. Thank you."

Nelson took the wine and I followed him to the back of the store. There was something peculiar about him that I noticed, not so out of character perhaps, because Nelson was an amiable man, but a rare restlessness that he showed. His speech was rapid and he moved almost clumsily.

"We'll take the stairs," he said. "That there is the elevator for Sally, if you're wondering. It's good for taking up groceries. I'll use it myself if I've had a long day."

Boxes of supplies lined the many shelves in the back. A small sink and counter with a coffee maker and those cups with the blowing and breaching whales, on hooks under a cupboard.

I followed Nelson up the steep staircase, tandem thumps of our heavy feet. Then a door opened and we were suddenly standing in his kitchen. A table set for three. I was surprised to see Sally standing by the stove. She wore braces on both her legs.

"Oh, Reuben, thanks for coming," she said. "I hope you like lasagne."

"Wonderful," I said. "I don't get to have that much anymore."

"Sally makes the best," Nelson said. "I'll open the wine."

I stood there in the kitchen while Nelson poured the wine. Sally must have noticed that I was looking at her braces.

"I can stand for a little while," she said. "I have to get out of the chair. My circulation's not that good anymore. And it's tiring to sit for a long time. I like to cook. And Nelson helps when he can. I wouldn't want it any other way. I'm fine, really. We have a good system. Nelson works the store and I man the radio. I would have said 'woman,' but it doesn't sound right." That sweet smile for me. "Glad you could come, Reuben."

"Thanks for inviting me," I said.

"Nelson, why don't you show Reuben my set-up in the living room," Sally said. "I'll call you when dinner's ready."

"Sure thing, Sal," Nelson said, handing me a glass of wine. "That's a fine colour, Reuben."

"I look after the culture in our family," Sally said playfully shaking her head.

"I just let you think that, Sal," Nelson bantered. "I know that I eventually have to drink it."

"He drinks cranberry tea in a clear glass mug because of the colour," Sally said. "One time in Victoria, we went into this fine tea shop. And Nelson asks the girl behind the counter, 'what do you have in reds?' Who does that, Reuben?"

Nelson just winked at me. The two of them seemed so happy to see me. I wondered about the things that I had constructed in my head, what kept me away. It all seemed such a waste, languishing over my doubts, creating things that had no real existence.

There in the living room the blinds were open with the view like the one below but with the true shape of the marina revealed by the elevation. A pattern of lights over the boats and the shimmering reflections in the water. The remnants of the day paled far out to sea and seemed like a sleepy eye. There was a telescope on a tripod ready by the window. But what caught my eye was the bank of computer monitors in one corner and a table against the window covered in maps with a line of books pushed against the pane, a mariner's library at hand's reach.

"This is where Sally does her work," Nelson said. "It's a little slow in the winter. You know, pleasure craft traffic goes down. But the emergency channel is on all the time. On the monitors there, you have your Marine Forecast, Weather Channel, Weather Network, CBC weather and Environment Canada and the Coast Guard. She goes over the satellite images. Records the conditions in a logbook. Always updates. You can never be sure now without the weather ships. You know yourself, Reuben, how the weather can change. So Sally uses all the devices she can find to help the boaters. The radio there goes out about 100 miles before another station picks up the boats. So this time of year we answer in-distress calls from any ship. There was a ferry once that went adrift south of Texada Island; we got a tug out there before she went aground. Sally loves the work. It gives her a good sense of purpose, you know, with her limitations. And she likes to watch the goings on around the marina. Up here in her perch."

"Like an eagle, I tell him, Reuben," Sally called out from the kitchen.

"And her hearing is just fine," Nelson said with the appropriate amplification.

"Dinner's ready, you two."

As we left the living room, I could feel the love between them and noticed the nest that they had made together, a television in the corner and a couch with soft fleece blankets, dolphins, and a pattern of orcas, of course. There was a lamp on a table made from a ship's wheel. Several pictures of Emily on the wall and paintings too, a schooner and ocean landscapes, eagles and ravens and a Haida paddle painted in reds and blacks. I imagined Nelson and Sally sitting there together, companions, friends, sharing their life by the sea, as intimate as wind and sail.

I sat down at the table with them. On each plate was a thick slab of lasagne, steaming and overwhelmed with melted cheese. It was a fine night, and I was grateful to be in their company. Imagine that, I thought, to be the main guest, the honoured guest. I felt so special, as if I mattered, mattered to them. And I moaned and I groaned because it tasted so good, that it felt so good. I could see that Sally was pleased. Nelson raised his glass to toast our health, and with that the talk settled and we ate. Then Nelson raised his glass once again and we toasted the good things in life, and to the good that was yet to come. It didn't seem to matter whether I believed in that or not, so present I was in that good-feeling place with Nelson and Sally.

We finished our dinner, having emptied the bottle of wine, and sat for a while contented. When the talk seemed to fade, I noticed a look between them and Nelson's tapping finger. I thought perhaps that I would think of something to say, something to nudge the conversation along, a return to the levity that filled that space just a short time before.

"That was sure good, Sally," I said. "I think that was the best lasagne I ever had. And the wine, Nelson, I will agree, had the most exquisite colour." I was certain that would start the charming banter between them. But there was nothing, only Sally's smile that had a queer tension running to Nelson. It startled me, a feeling that I had misspoken, that I had erred once again. Then I knew what it was. They had something to tell me.

"What is it?" I asked them. They turned to one another, not surprised by the question, but to defer to the other, how they should answer.

"There's something that we need to tell you, Reuben," Nelson said. "We just feel that we have to."

"It's about the boy," Sally said.

"Jonas?"

"Yes, Jonas."

"What about him? I don't understand."

"We had this feeling after that night in the snow," Nelson said, "when the Christmas lights were turned on. You remember, Reuben?"

"I remember," I said, listening intently now.

"Well, the kid was likeable enough," Nelson went on. "We thought that it wouldn't hurt for you to show him your boat. But it really wasn't our business, I must say. It was Sally who noticed something about him."

"It was partly the way he looked," Sally said. "He sure was a lovely boy. He had such compelling eyes. They make you want to stare at him. I'm sure that he was something with the girls at school. You just want to hug him. But later that night I was thinking about him. I remembered what Nelson had told me — why he came to Seaside — and why he always headed down to *my June*. I talked with Nelson about it. We talked long into the night. I'm sorry, Reuben. It sounds like so much meddling. It's not what we wanted to do. Since the boy was going home after you were to show him the boat, we just let it go. But then you see, you asked him back. You invited him back to sail. I guess we feel that you're better off without him."

"Why?"

"There could be something more, Reuben," Nelson said.

"Like what? What are you saying?"

"Nothing."

"Nelson, what the hell are you talking about?"

"Now, Reuben, we thought that you might have been wondering yourself. The way the kid was, I don't know. I think he had a crush on your wife. Kids can do that, but there could be more . . . I'm just saying, Reuben."

"What, that June was involved with him? Is that what you're saying, Nelson? My God, you invited me to dinner to tell me that?"

"Think about it, Reuben. Don't bring the kid back. Let him go. No good can come of it. It's an awful thing even to suggest it. We're sorry. But we couldn't see any other way."

"I don't believe what you're saying, Nelson. I know my wife. I know June!"

"I know. I know. But that night when I told him to be at your boat, just like you asked, well, he had an odd question."

"What?" I was reeling now, stunned, shocked at what I was hearing. The caving of my chest, folding inward, the coming implosion.

"He said, 'Does he know how much I love her?' I knew he wasn't talking about the boat. I never answered him right off. I was stunned by it, the way he asked it, in the present like. But it wasn't really a question. He was telling me. Then I said, 'why did you tell me that?' He just looked at me. There was something in his eyes that can tell you things. Not words but something else. You just know, like when you catch someone doing something they shouldn't be doing. He had that look. He had slipped and he knew it. But it wasn't really slipping. It was so matter of fact. Then something else. He laughed for no reason at all, laughed out loud with all the people holding their candles. We didn't know what to do, Reuben. We could be wrong. And I knew it could put something between us. I don't want that to happen. We've just got a bad feeling about that boy."

I got up from the table, an eruption in me, fighting the urge to heave it and all that was on it, so enraged I was, used like that by people who I thought were my friends. I felt a fool, betrayed and humiliated, to think that I was something. And I turned to them and their ashen faces twisted up to me, aghast at what they saw, the glut of my tears and my chin buckling against my words.

"Why would you do that to me, Nelson? Why?" And there came no answer. I turned and fled down the stairs like something scorched. Out into the hard street where all was bitter and dark.

The Inglorious
Spectacle of Confusion

∽

I WOULDN'T HAVE IT. I wouldn't acknowledge *him*. I wouldn't say his name out loud. *She wasn't like that*, I kept saying that over and over, a loop in my brain that kept me awake long into the night. How dare they suggest that? And now lying here with the first thoughts of the morning unravelling and rambling, I had to crawl out of bed, heave my legs into another day, lest I suffocate from recounting that injurious dinner with the Grommets. I willed my way to the bathroom and sat down to piss because I was too weary to stand.

When a man steps up to the mirror to shave, he will look and see what he has made of his life. There are times when he sees only a measure of his own reflection, so conditioned to clock time and duty, the morning parcelled out with the aim of punctuality. But when the work is all done, he will linger there awhile before his own judgement, a kind of lazy rumination. He cannot look into his own eyes for long without flinching from his regrets. But he will look and he will remember a life entire, all the joys and sorrows, the things that he didn't do and the things that he did, the shameful and the noble. But still inside him, just behind his grief, there exists that young man with a fist-full of courage and heart full of dreams.

I wanted him back. But I wondered if he ever existed at all? There was no *me* to hold on to, the vanquishing so sudden and complete. And yet it was that day, with Martin Rouse broken under my father's truck, that made *her* stop, brought her to me. My whole life surrendered to her in those moments in the shivering cold, yielded to something greater, an angel taking my hand, a promise never to let go. All who I thought I was existed in that union. It could not be extracted or removed or denied. June was everything. Her innocence needed no defence, needed no vindication. So why was I crazy with the words that spilled out of Nelson's mouth? I wanted to make him wrong, that he was mistaken, that I knew my own wife. How dare he.

I took her purse from the closet and set it down on the living room floor. It was curiously heavy. I sat in my chair and looked at it, the faux leather and champagne sparkle. I would start there, a reasonable thing to do, I thought. I was looking for nothing, expecting the benign and the harmless. There were so many things of June's that I hadn't touched. It never occurred to me that I had to remove them, pack up her life, that there was a time frame for such things. It crushed me to consider what that even looked like. Shirley told me that *life goes on*. But her life had been something of destruction, and her moving on, perhaps came like a prayer. I didn't want to hear those discouraging clichés. They were things said to be helpful, I suppose, but it meant nothing really, knew nothing of June and me, had no relative purpose other than to separate me from my life. The clothes and shoes and coats could wait until the summer, when the girls would come. But now the purse rested there before me with its mysteries, the private and proprietary things of a woman, a wife.

What was in it? How the mind grows suspicious without any real evidence, wants to make you work, conjures up the dramatic for its own sake. I didn't want to open it, finger through her things. It seemed so improper, dishonouring her that way. But when a thing is planted in the brain, it changes everything, sullies the sweetest stream. Oh, I could have chosen to ignore all that was said. Yes, it was all just a preposterous notion by the overzealous Grommets. But there would be no resolution in that, no closure for what they had set forth. The answer lay in finding nothing, just things a woman might use, nothing to stir a man.

I opened the clasp of the purse, undid the zipper and spilled all of its contents onto the floor. A thousand things tumbled down, an astounding store of shapes and objects, all familiar and unidentifiable from a casual glance. Just stuff, I was sure, without any real relevance. But I would sort through them, a dismal process of elimination. I felt like a prying bastard. I couldn't escape the thought that June was watching me somehow, horrified to see me on my knees. A disconcerting moment when I looked up to see just that, how she looked down at me from above the mantle, the girls too, all witness to my treachery. Nevertheless, I had to rationalize my circumstance, that I was alone, that everything was up to me now. What I was doing was an act of loyalty and love.

After a quick scrutiny I took the simple things that I knew, the lipstick and eyeliner and rounded compact with a mirror and brush, and set them to one side. June's wallet and a daytimer with yellow tabs were the largest items. I would look at them last. I hurried through the other things, sweeping them aside: the pens and pencils, paperclips, dimes and nickels and ubiquitous pennies, an Aspirin bottle, Kleenex, Tic Tacs and a comb with her hair still fastened to the teeth. I picked it up and touched the strands with my fingertips. Imagine that, her hair still so full of colour, a shining vitality.

All seemed as it looked, no more, no less, an accumulation inert and forsaken in the dark belly of a purse. I gathered what was left in my hand: receipts, a Stanley Theatre ticket stub. *Enchanted April* it read. I remembered that Sunday afternoon strolling along Granville Street in Vancouver with cherry blossoms falling on the sidewalks like pink snow. She was so happy. Then hidden under the tickets were two small square packages, flat, like those single-use towelettes. How strange to feel the ring through the package and the shocking label, *Blue Ram*, and such a jolt in my chest as I turned them over, not believing what I held in my hands, not understanding, not comprehending. There was only the shaking of my head. *Why would June have condoms in her purse?*

Then that moment when innocence departs, leaks through the crack of evidence, dismisses all that has been constructed and gives way to the mind in its full measure of misery. I brayed like a donkey, heaved my heartbreak there on my hands and knees until ropes of snot and tears fell in sheets from my battered face as if waxen and set ablaze. *Damn him. Damn him!*

I stayed there for a long time, unmoving, unthinking, in a state of annihilation where all meaning had died, down on the killing floor, until the light began to shift, the day moving on without me. At last I struggled to my feet, leaving the carnal heap on the floor and went into the kitchen and poured myself a glass of wine. I returned with the bottle and sat down in my chair. There in the farthest reaches of bewilderment, a man undone. My only comfort, the utility of alcohol and the coming fog. Soon I was able to reach down to the floor for the wallet and day-timer and set them on the table beside me. I waited for my courage, brainbound through my blood. I coaxed it now, poured my will down my throat.

It came warm and loath. Unable to handle another cruel discovery, I stood up from my chair. I reeled and seethed, something breaking inside me all at once, my jaw like iron and my teeth bared. I flung my rage across the room, smashed my glass of wine against the portrait on the wall. It bled there in English Bay, marred the innocent and the fool with his vision, the wine red and dripping down the mantle and a murderous splatter across the rug. "What have you done to us?" My shrill and tortured indictment.

Then silence hovered like death, and the darkness seeped in through the windows. But I was not alone. My anger was with me now, a companion that clung to the dark. It did not speak a language nor did it have a face. And I was not dead, because it needed life to exist. It needed me, to feed off my pain and to move me, push me toward the queer satisfaction of blame and guilt. I wasn't done. I had to know more.

I picked up June's wallet. There wasn't much in it except for several grocery store club cards, a Starbucks card, and a membership to her teacher organization tucked into the staggered slots meant for such things. Her driver's license, credit cards and debit card had all been cancelled shortly after her death. All the things needed for modern life were temporary after all. Even the graduation photos of the girls had lost their lustre. On the back of each were their names written in her hand. The ink with her life still in it. There was no anger there with those remote things, all decaying like something that had no more use. Just sadness now and its swift return, my blurred confusion swapping emotive ends.

June's day timer for 2012–13 was a full year of appointments, mostly around school: exams and marking, staff meetings, parent/teacher interviews, seminars and conferences. Such a full professional life. Some entries were more personal. Lori and Mandy's birthdays. And mine too, included in her scholastic world. Dinner at the Tomato Café at 7:00, our favourite spot to unwind from the rigors of public life. On the weekends it would say, gardening or sailing. How did life go on without her?

Near the end of the school term one name appeared on the calendar. It was not a name. It was the letter J, but a name to me, as if it were written in full. Then it appeared regularly, that letter and a time. I thumbed through the pages, the repetition. There loose along the spine like an oversight was a yellow note with that same irrefutable J and a telephone number. I was wild with fervent impulses, drunk to be sure, and not fit to pick up the telephone.

I dialled the number and didn't care what was to come. There was only discovery now and truth, accusations ready and dripping off my tongue. But of course it rang and rang and went to voicemail. I waited for his voice, tried to remember it, the inflection when he told me about his mother that morning aboard *my June*. But it never came.

Hi, this is Judy, leave a message.

I wasn't prepared for a woman's voice, its brusque command. I fumbled, panicked. "This is Reuben . . . Sorry, I was looking for Jonas," I said like an idiot, and then quickly hung up.

The Reading

WHEN I AWOKE in the morning I felt abandoned by the only thing that I possessed, June's memory. I was angry and hurt. My mind launched its charges of betrayal as a matter of default. It seemed there was no way to resolve my suspicions, so powerful and compelling the evidence. But something wanted expression, my unconscious primal defence. I masturbated in the shower because I didn't want to believe it was true, that it had something to do with me. The gesture of a man with a singular spasm of fleeting pleasure, and then the shame and confusion of himself in the mirror. What did it prove?

I was running out of friends. Nelson was no friend. He had set in motion something that I could not stop, the master himself with his *ripples*, a man I trusted, who had fatted me for the slaughter. And Shirley somewhere in Africa sorting out her life, perhaps never to return. That left Muirgheal. But it was not her friendship that I sought. No, it was what she might know, some power she possessed. It said so on her business card. I was hardly a believer in such things, the unproven spectral realms, speaking to the dead, although I will admit my many conversations with June since she died. But a man can only drink so much wine and languish in the mind's conventions, a bitter world full of shadow. A psychic reading could be no worse. And I couldn't forget how composed she was at the Grief Group. She had a certain quality that moved me. She was no fabrication. But how much to tell her? How could I speak to a part of myself that was disappointed in a wrong number?

I parked out on the street that evening. Rare stars blinked against the infinite black dome of the world and a mild breeze moved the banners. Soon they would be replaced with spring banners and Seaside would awaken from its long winter slumber. But the spring would also bring Jonas. What to do with him?

The bookstore was closed and I had to knock. I looked around. There was no one on the street. I was nervous that I might be seen, marked as the fanciful naïve. I don't know why I cared so much. So many things no longer mattered. How swiftly the lesser problems fall away against a force that threatens identity and sanity. And then she came floating from the back in her scarves and shawl and opened the door.

"Come on in, Reuben," Muirgheal said. "This is a bit of a surprise, I must say."

"Well, for me too," I said, following her.

She led me to the back of the bookstore and pulled a curtain of beads aside where a door had once been, revealing a tiny room filled with florid light and faint lingering incense. The flame from a candle moved in a slow dance. There were two wicker chairs that faced each other and a wicker table between. On the walls, paintings of angels and faeries. Dreamy music played soft and hypnotic. We sat in the chairs, and she folded her hands expectantly. There I was, sitting across from another woman. She was covered up to her neck, no distractions tonight. It all seemed so strange and alien to me, a bit too weird and unearthly. I wondered what truth could be foretold, what things could be known about my life in that enigmatic cube. I decided that I would not tell her a thing about Jonas. The sceptical part of me wanted to leave nothing to chance.

Then all at once the room seemed to fill with her presence, a delicate light about her head.

"You have come for answers," she said. It was not a question.

"There are things that I don't understand."

"You would like help with that?"

"Yes. I don't know what else to do."

"The desperate come to me. And those who want to know what's in store for them."

"Their futures."

"Yes, we all want to know if our lives are going to be all right. If our dreams will come true."

"Can you do that?"

"I sense things. They come as glimpses into the future. Perhaps I do know what is coming. I have felt this many times. But how can you tell someone that his or her dreams are all but over? It is a cruel business when all they want to hear is the good news."

"So you don't tell them."

"What I can do, Reuben, is help them see for themselves."

"You might know something, but you wouldn't tell me?"

"I will guide you to a future that already exists."

"It all sounds so vague."

"I'm sure there is a clairvoyant or seer who will tell you a future that would please you. They guess based on certain clues that you give them from selected questions. They are frauds. They seek out the weak and vulnerable. How easy it is to offer a hopeful future to someone who is afraid. If I was such, you could imagine how long I would last in a small town. I would have been out with the first tide."

"I suppose that's what I'm afraid of. If I ask you a specific question, then I might not know if your answer is truth or deception."

"This happens all the time. A client will come in and tell me nothing. It is their way of knowing if what I tell them is true for them."

"I have a situation that I need help with. I don't need to contact my wife June to see if she's all right. Nothing like that. But you see, it does involve her. And I will admit that I don't want to say too much. I am like your other clients. I want to think, *wow*, how did she know that? She couldn't have known that without some kind of power or psychic ability. Whatever it is. That's all."

"Then sitting here I sense there is something that is not right. It's not the way you thought it was. That is why you are here."

"That's true."

"But it is more than that. It is a matter of innocence or guilt."

"Yes."

"This is what you want to know."

"I need to know. My whole life . . ."

"Innocence and guilt do not exist on their own. How could I know what is innocence, what is guilt?"

"But you must know, if you can see what happened."

"Whenever we declare who is guilty, we are convinced of their transgressions. This person did that and that person did this."

"Yes, that very thing. You know what I'm talking about. You know who is guilty."

"How could I know this?"

"Because you're a psychic. Isn't that what you do?"

"I know what can be revealed."

"You can tell me. I don't care if it's not good."

"Reuben, let me explain. Guilt and innocence have no objective reality. They're always defined by someone. The world is rife with the guilt of others. Governments declare guilt based on rules, laws. It is always someone's judgement. Actions and conduct are subject to judgement. Perhaps it is the way that society controls its population. The guilty have wronged and the innocent have not. Punish the guilty, revere the innocent."

"I guess that I want you to be specific."

"To declare someone guilty is to know every moment that has led to that declaration. Every thought, every circumstance, every influence in their lives, every joy and tragedy, everything that shapes a human being, what can be seen as guilt, perhaps can be viewed with compassion and understanding. Perhaps we can never know enough about another."

"I don't know about that."

"We all have been both guilty and innocent. We may not have wanted to hurt anyone, but we did. As children we were innocent, before we learned the ways of the world, how to judge, and what was good or bad. But who knows what is good or bad?"

"I think that I do. I know what is good and bad. I learned that much in this life. I was like most kids of my generation. Be good or else."

"I know that is true. There was a great shame then. We stopped being children and became what our parents wanted us to be. It created guilt in us where it should not have existed."

"All right. Perhaps you don't have an answer to my question."

"What I can tell you, Reuben, is that your problem is not what it seems. This I know."

"What do I do with that?"

"There are other entities that could assist you, energies that exist outside of your awareness."

"Like what?"

"We can feel them through an insight, something that we suddenly realize, our intuition. It could be from a song on the radio that has meaning for us. It could be a sign in a window meant for us. It could be a number sequence that catches our attention. Something that is repeated, a word or a letter. We just need to be open to receiving the many messages. They may come from strangers, friends, anyone. Just imagine that you are a receiver, like a satellite dish."

"That's a little hard to accept."

"I can only lead you into your own life. No one knows more about yourself than you do."

"Well, all right. I guess I'm on my own."

"We're never alone, Reuben."

"You seem so convinced."

"Our souls have many lifetimes, many personalities that exist all at once. There is no time. I have memories of my lifetimes. I could ask you to trust me. But why would you? You are on a journey. I can only point to the direction, not the way of your path."

"Can you do one thing for me?"

"If I can."

"Tell me something about my past that no one knows about."

"You don't trust me."

"I need to know. I want to trust. I do."

Then Muirgheal reached out and took my hands. "Close your eyes and empty your thoughts," she said.

Her hands were warm. I tried not to think sitting there in the dark. I could hear her breathing, long and steady breaths as if she were concentrating. The only sound was our inhalations and exhalations. The music had disappeared. I wondered if it had been there at all. Then she released my hands and began to speak. I opened my eyes.

"She came to you," she said haltingly. "Without name or introduction, she found you, as she had done many times before. A time when carnage and death visited the winter, when the snows were deep and many perished. She came to care for the dying, to bless them as they passed on. And she tended to those who survived. Many times you were lost, and so it was that you were found. She will find you again."

I sat there listening to the tale. Some vague familiarity, I couldn't be sure. Her voice seemed to change, as an interpreter translates one language to another, one lifetime to another. I played along. "So what did she want from me?"

"Your strength."

"My strength? She was the strong one."

"You see, Reuben, things aren't what they seem. You survived while others did not. You do not see this as strength. Can you see it now in this lifetime?"

"I don't know. I guess not."

"Did you find your answer?"

"I probably have more questions."

"The answers are waiting."

"So, this seems more like a counselling session than a reading."

"Is there a difference?"

We sat a moment. I wanted to ask her about Jonas now. But I knew the question could not be answered. What would she have said, really? I didn't believe that Muirgheal would have said anything to hurt me. She was guarding something, protecting the truth perhaps. Then why provide readings at all? She said as much at the beginning of the session.

Had I come to the wrong place, seeking something that could not be sought? Then I could hear the music once again, that ethereal accompaniment in the chamber. It was not music really, more like singing, voices rising and falling, a song to make you weep.

The session ended. Muirgheal led me out of the room to the front counter. I handed her the fee and thanked her. She was quiet. That old feeling of mine, that it was something I said. But then she smiled warmly and touched my arm.

"I think I've found your book," she said. "I put a hold on it."

"*Moby Dick*?"

"Yes, an estate sale in San Diego. They want $1500. And I need to add 10% for my commission."

"That's a lot for a book."

"It's an old book, Reuben. I think it's what you wanted."

"Yes, all right. Thank you."

"Drop off a cheque and I'll confirm the sale."

"I'll do that."

Out in the street everything was the same. The banners still moved against the stars. Just then it seemed time had stopped.

Down at the Sand Dollar Café

I COULD SEE MY neighbours Bert and Rollie waving at me when I walked through the door of the Sand Dollar Café to get a coffee for my walk. They were with another man at a table, sharing breakfast and a laugh. I had heard them from out in the street and thought I would say hello. Three white-haired guys trying to make sense of their lives. At least they were laughing. I waved back, a sociable smile. But I didn't want to sit with them. That much of a good time made me feel nervous. I know it's hard to believe. You would think that it would be a remedy for sorrow or other miserable states. I told the waitress I would be a minute and walked over to be polite.

"Hey, Reuben," Bert said.

"How's it goin', Reuben?" Rollie said.

"Sit down," the other man said. He had a loud voice and a great sweeping moustache. It so overwhelmed his mouth that you couldn't see his lips move. "Do you golf?" he asked me.

"Reuben's not a golfer," Bert said.

"Then what do you do if you don't golf?" the man said, chuckling. He looked familiar. "I didn't think there's anything else worth living for," he added with a flourish of bravado.

It was all a joke to him. I had him for a loud mouth. He laughed a bit too hard at my expense, and I could see that it bothered Rollie. He came to my rescue.

"Reuben's a walker, Councillor Porter," he said. "He loves to walk. Up and down all these streets."

"Yeah," Bert said, "I could use the exercise myself." He placed his hands on his great paunch.

I appreciated what Bert and Rollie were trying to do. They were good neighbours, but I wasn't going to sit down with that asshole councillor.

I heard the door open behind me and someone come into the café. When I turned, I saw it was Nelson Grommet. He looked different wearing a baseball hat but the councillor recognized him. He said something under his breath that he shouldn't have.

"Look at that, there's that bloodsucking marina operator," he said. "The prick took my boat out." He glared now. "That son of a bitch's not sitting here."

"Hey, pal," I said jerking my head to him, "shut your mouth. That's my friend you're talking about!" I startled myself for standing up for Nelson like that. It came out of nowhere. Bert and Rollie must have been wishing that they were out with their dogs when the councillor pushed back his chair.

"Easy now, Councillor Porter," Rollie said.

"Sit down," Bert said.

He was a big man when he stood, with a massive chest and a neck like my thigh. He had a knotted ponytail at the back of his head and gave the impression that he might have been a World Wrestler at one time. He held his arms out from his sides as if he were about to draw his guns on me. I imagined he would have been a formidable opponent when he was younger. I couldn't make such a claim for myself. After Martin Rouse was killed I always felt that my life should be compliant and agreeable. I wanted to be passive, non-existent, someone who didn't matter. I wanted to be invisible. And I knew I wasn't going to lick that councillor. Oh, I could feel my fists curl and my poor racing heart. He certainly pissed me off; a Seaside elected official talking about one of its own citizens like that. But if he hit me, he just might kill me.

I glanced around to weigh my options. The waitress was watching from the till, and Nelson looked on holding two coffees in his hands. He didn't seem quite sure what the fuss was all about. Rollie with his police experience tried to calm the councillor and stood between us. I was sure that Rollie wouldn't let anything get out of hand.

But it seemed Councillor Porter had a temper. He began to paw at me, trying to sucker me into a fight. "Come on," he sneered, "let's see what you've got?"

I didn't have the size or the experience to get into a scrap. A shocking thing to have someone in your face at my age, but I could still sling a word or two. I didn't have much time to come up with something for him. It had to be something that would agitate him into submission. It was a long shot at best. I knew he was waiting for me to throw a right hand. Then there it was right in front of me. I pointed to it. "Aren't you worried that your squirrel will shit in your mouth?" I said as coolly as I could.

That did it, except for the submission part. He lunged at me with a clutching hand, fury and indignation in his beet-red face and his eyes white and flaring. But he was top-heavy and fell over Rollie's leg, striking his chin on the back of a chair. It was an awful whack that split it like a spare grin. He ended up on his back like a turtle, bleeding onto the floor. His eyes seemed loosened in his head as he searched for me in their contrary orbits. I could see he had no idea where I was, or where he was for that matter. I thought I might have killed him with my salvo. A moment later, the waitress rushed over with a towel, and Bert helped him onto a chair. I was surprised to see that Nelson had been standing right behind me as Rollie guided me away from the mess toward the door.

"Sorry about all that, Reuben," Rollie said. He was laughing like hell. "Councillor Porter is a bit of a hot head. But damn it, that was funny."

Once I had left the café and was standing on the sidewalk, Nelson came out behind me. I was trembling, a terrible cold up my back, with the sun warm and full in the street.

"Bought you a coffee," Nelson said.

"Thanks," I said. I took it and pried open the lid and slurped off the hot slick.

"Just the way you like it, Reuben."

It was odd standing there with Nelson. I noticed his baseball hat. It was the Jays. "How did you know I would be in there?"

"I've been looking for you."

"Yeah." We started walking.

"The councillor there is no stranger to a fray," he said, "and he's partial to the sound of his own voice. What started it?"

"He asked me if I golfed."

"That'll do it."

"He doesn't like you much."

"Yeah, I heard that."

"He shouldn't have said it."

"He's still sore at me. That boat of his was leaking oil and fuel, fouling the other boats. He wouldn't do the repairs so I had to take it out myself. Then he wouldn't pay for the cleanup. So I rented his berth. Just business. A councillor should know better."

"God, I'm still shaking," I said. I was without my little white pills, and not a bottle to douse the white flares of my fright. That big bastard would have a scar to remember me by, down at the Sand Dollar Café where old men played like boys.

"You did good, Reuben. You're just a little shocky. It might be helpful to walk a spell."

Nelson must have heard everything after all, watched as I defended him. It's a telling thing in a man when he reacts without thinking, some truth that endures, that needs to be upheld. I never thought I would be out walking with him. He was always parked behind the counter down at the marina. I was still upset with him, the things that he said, his assumptions, but just then I was glad to be with him. It didn't seem rational or even possible that very morning. But there we were sharing a coffee as if nothing at all had come between us. Our walking took us past the town hall with its daffodils in the planters. They faced the sun so full of hope with their impossible yellow blooms. Then we neared the water and Nelson pointed down the promenade.

"That's the tonic," he said, "to be out along the sea."

"What about the marina?"

"At breakfast Sally commented that I was sulking. 'Go find him,' she said."

The promenade was constructed of paving stones. Many Seaside residents were out walking along the easy grade on that first warm day of spring. There was a breeze coming off the water. It had the smell of a fresh new world. I was aware of Nelson and his waddling gate, the side-to-side motion of his old hips. He was mechanical as we went along, stiff, and pointing up the hillside to the finches in the blackberries, then down along the beach where winter storms left great heaps of latticed logs. As we walked along, the expanse of sea and sky restored me, allowed my eyes to settle upon the benign. It made me forget for a while.

Soon the pointing was done and the last robin had posed with its fine terracotta breast. We stopped at a lookout where a wooden bridge crossed a gully. We rested our elbows on the railing and finished our coffee. We watched a solitary eagle on the beach ignore the torment of crows. I waited for him.

"We're sorry, Reuben," Nelson said as I knew he would. "We're sorry as hell."

"It was hard," I said.

"Sometimes a man will say something and regret it but can't stuff it back in his mouth."

"I get sick thinking about it."

"I wish you could forget that night, Reuben."

"I have my doubts, you know."

"Yeah."

"I found something. I can't tell you what it is. And I don't know what to do now."

"Jesus, Reuben."

"I went to see Muirgheal."

"The lady at the bookstore."

"Yes, I went to her for one of those psychic readings. But it sounded a lot like nothing."

"Sal went once," Nelson said.

"Really?"

"Yeah, Muirgheal told her something that'll give you shivers. She said that Emily wanted her mom to know she didn't blame her for giving her the front seat. You see, Emily wanted to sit in the front with me. I remember she was quite persistent about it, you know, the way kids can be. So Sally sat in the back and Emily hopped in the front. The car hit us right where Emily was sitting. No one but us knew that. Gives me chills just telling it."

"That's something all right," I said with the fine hairs erect on my neck as Nelson had predicted. "It makes you wonder, but I just don't know. She never told me much. She said something about sharing lifetimes."

"Who can say, Reuben? I can tell you that losing a child changes a lot of things. Just not black and white anymore."

At this, Nelson turned to me in that thoughtful way of his, with his sorrow and regret plain in his face. The creases in his skin seemed deeper. He looked older and not so durable. I thought that perhaps he was waiting for something else, that one thing I said I had found. Then I noticed his baseball hat, the stylized J on the peak. He watched me.

"Spring training," he said. "I love the Blue Jays. I brought a television down so I can watch the games."

He looked off now. I guess he realized that I wasn't going to say much more. He hung his head for a moment then turned back to me, his old hands folded on the railing. Nelson Grommet was deliberating.

"I was looking at my surveillance videos," he said after a minute. "That kid came down to your boat thirteen times. A few times just before the sun came up. Other times in the dark. One time he seemed to drop to his knees. Another time he paced up and down the dock. I don't know what it means, Reuben. But the boy's not right."

"Something about the boat, Nelson. It doesn't make sense."

"Maybe it was the boat after all. I thought you needed to know."

"I'm glad you told me. I have to resolve this. I can't take much more of it. The speculation's making me mad."

"He's coming soon."

"In two weeks."

"What are you going to do?"

"I could let him come," I said. "See how it goes."

"Confronting him could be a problem."

"Perhaps I could let him tell me."

"Might be tricky."

"One way or the other, I'll be done with it."

We walked back as friends once again, with our stiff but measured strides that had managed to bring us that far. He came to find me that day, came to heal a bitter wound with his own humility. How he walked me through the processes of reconciliation with his simplicity, pausing to hear birdsong, allowing life to flow through him like a flute. Nelson Grommet was an unremarkable man. But he had a remarkable sense of reliability. One day I would have to tell him about what I did, tell him that I killed a boy. I wasn't so worried about what he would say, what he would think of me. I knew now that I could entrust the truth to him. I had only to trust myself.

"I wish my oldest brother Walter had been in there with me," I said.

"Brothers are good for such things. They always have your back."

"Walter was like that."

"That councillor wasn't going to hurt you, Reuben. He was about to wear a cup of hot coffee."

Closing the Distance

◇

THE FAIR WEATHER brought the sailors out, drove them down to the marina where the sun burned away the damp and funk of winter. Everyone on the dock milled about the boats, taking up old conversations and comparing how their boats fared against a succession of storms that had slapped the west coast for nearly six months. Many boats were being taken out of the water, with Nelson working twelve-hour days setting them on chocks and inspecting the hulls and keels. He would check the rudders and propeller shafts, inspect for saltwater corrosion on anything metal, and then run his hands over the fibreglass that was normally hidden below the watermark. A great preparation was underway as the days grew warmer, with the swallows home at last, arcing and dipping in their number above the marina. It was the sea that brought them all, to sail upon it, to feel the spray, and the tilting of decks.

I was down at the boat most days now, studying the handbooks, the details of sailing, tides and charts, plotting courses, windward and down-wind, and of course, the wardrobe of sails — a suite for every breeze. Like a student I was, learning all over again. But now I was going to be the teacher. I went about the spars and rigging, lubricated the stays and wires and varnished the wood planking on the deck, brushing and scrubbing the fittings and plates. Down below, I washed every corner and resealed every seam. There were only the sails now to bring down. All was ready for Jonas. There would only be the teacher and the student, and my fierce and utter vigilance. I would watch him and I would listen. I would find him in his weakness, catch the failing in his eyes, the hesitation and wavering of his words. He would reveal to me the very truth, the things that only he could know.

It was a good place to be, waiting for Jonas. He had called on the telephone and said he had bought a car and would arrive on the coming Monday afternoon. As the very thought of his arrival made my stomach sour, I kept occupied with the boat, reading *Moby Dick* when I had a moment to spare and wondering when Melville was going to get to the white whale.

I sat on the deck on a lawn chair that I had brought down, taking in the sounds, watching the people giddy with expectation. Now and then I would see Nelson. He was always at a different place, in and out of the store, dispensing gas to the boats, hauling out and hauling in. And he wasn't a young man, I kept on thinking. Those rusty hips of his were likely bone on bone by now. Coming down the dock, he looked like a veteran of the bronc-riding circuit. But he never complained. He just kept going, always watching for me, so attentive he was now, as if my guardian sworn. He would be out among the boats on his rounds and he would come to me, never to another seafarer. It was a privilege to be under the care of Nelson Grommet.

On one particular day, I looked up to see what I took to be the figure of a stranger standing against the sun. I shaded my eyes with my hand to see more clearly. He was a large man and it gave me a sudden start, as it seemed just then that Councillor Porter had come to pay me a visit to enact his revenge. But no, it was not the peevish councillor. Nelson would never have allowed him to set foot in the marina. I knew this man, and how impossible it was to be looking into his aging face. My whole life flashed before my eyes, so swift and incomprehensible the drift of years, compressed to a space between my breaths. It was Walter.

"Walter, what are you doing here?" I said standing and coming to the deck rail.

"Can I come aboard?" he said.

"Yes, sure."

He was heavy now and laboured over the railing onto the deck. I offered him my chair and he sat heavily. He seemed breathless. It was not a happy visit, I could see. There had been no warm embrace between us, no gesture, not a handshake. He had not come to catch up on our lives, or even to make things right between us. He was there with the duty that followed him all his life.

"So what brings you to Seaside?" I asked. I sat on the plank benching.

"I'll get to the point, Reuben," he said. "I had to put Lyle in a home."

"What?"

"He has some form of dementia." He folded his hands over his stomach.

"My God, Walter. When did this happen?"

"It had been coming for a while."

"I had no idea. Why didn't you tell me?"

"Well, you have your life," he said. His eyes were deep and pinched cold, a bloodless face.

"What do you mean by that?"

"Look, Reuben, after Mom and Dad died, you pretty well disappeared," he said leaning forward. "I tried to keep the family together. But, you know, you had that big house in Kerrisdale. Let's face it; you had a lot of money. Not like us rural folks. You didn't give a shit about us. I carried Lyle on my fucking back for most of his life. Where were you? I tried to keep him working at the garage, but he kept screwing up. He was drunk half the time. And yeah, he managed a girlfriend or two, but he couldn't keep a relationship for long. You know Lyle, that wit of his, that charm. When the laughing stopped, they found themselves staring at a drunk."

"You still blame me, don't you?" How he just came out with it. He didn't seem to care what he said.

"It would have been a lot different if you hadn't hit that kid."

"But I did. Damn it, Walter!"

"It seems to me that you washed your hands of us."

"That's not true."

"I think that it was June. She never wanted to come to Ladner. It was like the fucking Ozarks to her."

"Walter, what the hell's the matter with you? You come all this way to vent all your shit on me? Jesus, June's dead. Why would you say that?"

"Because it's true. Hey, I'm just filling you in, Reuben. I came by to tell you how the rest of your family's been doing. The wife and kids are fine, if you care to know. I'm still working at the garage. Can you believe it? A lifetime of filthy fucking hands. Look at them. There's no retirement for me. Just like the old man. And Lyle's probably pissing himself right about now. They'll need to change his diaper. I did that. I did all that, Reuben. He couldn't live in his apartment anymore. They evicted him. You should have seen that place. Oh, yeah, you wouldn't have wanted to. You would have been too busy!"

"You never asked me. How do you know what I would have done?"

"Why do you always have to be asked? You have a telephone!"

"This is not fair. I don't deserve this! Why don't you just go home, Walter?"

He lowered his head, and as he did so, his anger seemed to deflate. "You're right. I'll go."

"Why did you really come?"

"I don't know. I have something for you. I don't know why I brought it. It was stupid."

"What is it?"

"Donny Rouse came to see Lyle," he said. "And Lyle knew who it was. It was so strange, this old guy, like you or me. Lyle was sitting in his room, and Donny took Lyle's hand, held it and wept. I couldn't believe it. It made me angry at first. You bastard, I thought, you could have killed him or any one of us. But things change. People change. He asked Lyle to forgive him. And you know, with all his problems, his failing health, all his dreams that never came true, Lyle had something. He forgave him. Right there. I never thought something like that was possible. And

Donny Rouse forgave you, Reuben, for killing his brother. He wanted me to tell you that. That's why I came. I thought you might want this." Walter reached into his coat pocket and handed me an envelope.

I opened it. It was the card that Carol Rouse had sent to our mother when she was dying. It was yellowed and frayed at the corners, but there were still the flowers in a meadow, and inside, her handwriting, a tender plea for forgiveness.

"You kept this?"

"It was stuffed into a box all these years. I'm the keeper of the family archives. I never thought it would happen, that Donny Rouse would show up. It almost didn't. We're all getting older. It took a lot of guts for him to do that."

"But you can't forgive me."

"It doesn't come easily for me. All this forgiveness, what's the point of it? Everybody forgiving everybody. I'm bitter. I'll probably die bitter. I'm not going to lie about it."

"You sound so sure."

"I'm just tired. I should go. I have to book into a motel for the night."

"We can stay on the boat."

"I don't think so."

"I've got a bottle of wine in the galley. Have a drink."

"I don't know, Reuben."

"Have a drink, and then go . . . if you have to."

"Yeah, well, I suppose that I can do that."

I went down into the galley and poured two glasses of wine and returned to the deck. Walter was standing, looking around the marina, to the forested mountains and to the boats brilliant in their berths. They were things he could never have, a place that was beyond him. He liked what he saw. How a brother arrives after all those years and can do nothing but rage against the things he doesn't understand. He didn't really know me, what my life had been like. I had killed Martin Rouse. It seemed somehow that I wasn't permitted to suffer for what I had done. There was no clemency allotted to me, no recognition of why I had to stay away. There was nothing that I could say to convince him of why I had to choose June's hand. Who could understand such a thing? But I had left, slipped away from them in the night. It was not rejection, but an act of compassion for myself, for them. And yes, Walter stayed, remained to hold together the friable parts of a family. How could I be angry with him? What could I say to him, so full of his acrimony and unlived passions?

We sat a moment in the stillness that comes with a boat. It moves and it speaks, and the silent listening arises unbidden. Walter sat there with his hands around his glass, those working hands that could crush it if he wasn't careful. He had our father's hands. How serious he was. He had always been that way, the dependable one. It didn't seem fair. With the sun on him, the Walter of my youth was scarcely there at all, hardly recognizable now. But he was still there in his eyes, the boy I had looked up to. Eyes never seem to change. It was there where I would find him.

"You've got a fine set-up here, Reuben," he said. "I left my car at your house. Your neighbour said where you'd be. Nice little town. It reminds me of Ladner."

"Yes." There was little for me to say. I recognized we were at a crossroad as brothers, something to salvage and heal, or perhaps only to reconfirm the distance between us.

His eyes were working now. He was taking it all in, relaxing back in his chair, unwinding — and something else. He did not want to quit on me.

"I guess I was practising what I would say to you for a long time," he said. "I feel a bit foolish now."

"Don't be," I said.

"I was a little hard on you."

"Yes, you were. But thanks for the card."

"I figured it would mean something to you."

"And you."

He nodded. "You know, sometimes at the garage, I look up from what I'm doing, and I have this deep sadness. It feels like regret. Standing there surrounded by tools and broken-down cars. I know I can't stop. I would die within a year. It happens to half the men my age. Why would I resent all this?"

"You're sitting here right now with me, having a glass of wine. That's not too bad."

"Not too bad at all. Never had time to myself. I guess this is it." He raised his glass.

Just then Nelson came up alongside the boat. He was out on his rounds. "Hey, Reuben," he said.

"Hi, Nelson, this is my brother Walter," I said to him.

Walter stood up and moved to the side of the boat and reached up and shook Nelson's hand. "Pleased to meet you," he said.

"Hello, Walter," Nelson said. "Reuben was telling me about you."

"Yeah, what did he say?"

"Oh, some fellow took exception to Reuben's golf game a week or so ago and wanted to teach him a lesson. He said that he wished you were there with him. Anyway, nice meeting you, Walter, got to go sell something."

We watched Nelson head up the dock. Walter was curious, I could see.

"Nelson owns the marina," I told him. "He's always coming by to see me."

"Who was this guy?" he said.

"Some loud mouth. I think he wanted to kill me."

"All you had to do was call, Reuben. I would have been there in a heartbeat."

"I know, Walter."

"I'm sorry I wasn't there for you when June died. No excuse for it."

"It's all right. Thanks for looking after Lyle."

"It's not the life he wanted."

"No, it wasn't."

"You can stay with us, you know. Come to Ladner once in a while. See Lyle."

"Yes, I'll do that." I heard the disingenuous sound of my voice and felt bad for it.

"Don't wait too long, Reuben."

We finished the bottle of wine in the late afternoon and then warmed some beef stew from a can. We watched the sun set. And when the stars emerged over the green-black mountains, we drank tea and were speechless. We stayed over in the boat that night, slept in sleeping bags. I couldn't tell Walter about Jonas. He didn't need to know. He still carried the burden of our family, and that would have been just too much for him. So he would finish what our father began, what I couldn't do. He was chosen for it. He returned to Ladner.

I reflected for days after that on what really brought Walter to Seaside. He had brought me the card that Carol Rouse had given our mother. That was thoughtful. I placed it on the dresser in my bedroom. The news of Lyle was sad indeed, and yes, I had to know. It was hard for me to imagine a visit from Donny Rouse. There were many reasons, some he explained to me so vehemently that day on the boat. I wondered if he came just to see me. He could have called and simply mailed the card. Perhaps he looked up from his tools and broken-down cars and remembered that I never intended to kill Martin Rouse. He might have heard our father, who I was certain still had a presence in the garage. He might have heard our mother's tender prodding. All perhaps true, but I believe Walter felt the passage of time in his bones, a sudden hard realization for a man. He just wanted to make things right.

The Offer

◌℘◌

NELSON OPENED THE store just after the sun came up. I had my coffee at my usual table early so I could spend some time talking with him. He seemed to appreciate it. Soon he would be called down to the gas pumps or up to the yard to meet with an anxious boat owner wondering when he could sail. It was worth seeing Seaside at that time of day. The sunrises in the east nearly matched the sunsets in the west. It was always mirrored in the water, where heaven met Earth, the transformation of light into fluid, the tangible sea ablaze — the heralding and the fulfillment.

"See the cormorants there, Reuben, sitting on the pilings," Nelson said pointing out the window. He leaned over the counter. "They look like sun worshippers with their wings out drying like that. People aren't much different. Every spring they want the sun. Most of them sit all day on their decks. Never leave the marina. It's a fine way to spend a day.

Just like you and your brother. It feels as though you've done something, as if you've been somewhere. I'm here all day long and haven't sat on a boat for more than a minute."

I watched the cormorants, motionless in their black capes. I liked the way Nelson asked a question sometimes, when he wasn't sure what the answer might be. It would come clothed in a story. "You can stay as long as you want on my boat," I said.

"That's it, Reuben, I can only sit a minute."

"You're all over the place. Maybe you need help."

"I don't know. It's hard to find good help. The kids like being near the water but they never last. You're always training them. I don't mind teaching the young ones. I don't. I would just like someone more reliable."

"You would?"

"Just sayin', Reuben. I have to depend on someone. Sometimes I have to take Sal to the doctor in Powell River or Vancouver."

"You want someone who's mature."

"Yeah, mature, that's the word."

"With experience."

"That's the thing, Reuben. You don't need experience if you're mature and responsible. Folks like that just figure it out. That's what I'm looking for."

"So, you're looking for someone?"

"I suppose I could use someone. Yeah."

"Part time?"

"Well, I think so. Just to help out."

"So what would this person look like?" I asked, playing along with him now.

"I suppose he would be retired and open to the possibility of working again. You know, about your age. And maybe someone in pretty good shape. Looks after himself. I think he should have thin white hair, no offense, Reuben, and well, someone who's willing to start early and doesn't mind discussing the state of the world. And something else."

"What's that?"

"He has to like my coffee."

"I like the whale mugs," I said. "I like the orcas; that's my favourite."

"Close enough," he said.

"That's the damnedest job offer that I've ever had," I cackled. I appreciated Nelson's light-hearted banter more than ever now. I could feel the world closing in around me, like those walls you see in movies, narrowing, threatening to crush me. More than ever, my life felt destabilized, absent of meaning. But things were coming to a head.

"No pressure, Reuben. I know that the kid's coming today. So maybe you could help out after you're done with him. I just want you to know that whatever happens, you have a place here."

"I never thought I would ever work again. I don't need the money."

"It's more than the money. I don't have to work. We get offers for this place all the time. But money can't buy what a man feels about himself. If he's not sitting on top of a mountain in some ashram, he still wants to make his own way. I always feel better after I've accomplished something. Just doing something with my hands. And working up there with her marine radio is everything to Sally. Just sayin', Reuben."

"That's a pretty good pitch there, Nelson. Have you been working on that awhile?"

"No, I wasn't trying to do anything, really. Thought that I would give you the opportunity. That's all, Reuben. After a while things can just stop coming our way, and people too. We might just give up."

"Yes, it had been a while since I saw my brother Walter."

"I thought so. My brothers died before we could get together. Time ran out. We waited too long. I often wondered what we were waiting for. We just let things stay between us. Stubbornness is not something a man will admit to sometimes. It's hell on families."

"You could have just come out and asked me. You know, do you want a job?"

"You might have just said no. There'd be no fun in that. And you pretty well made the case for me, Reuben. I appreciate that." He laughed, trying hard to fortify me.

"I don't know, Nelson. I'm having a hard enough time just sitting here waiting."

"I think you have a lot of courage, Reuben."

"I don't feel so brave."

"Yeah, well, that's a troubling thing not to know what's ahead of you."

"I'm not troubled, I'm scared shitless."

"I know it."

"How will I know what to do?"

"Just let it happen. You'll know, Reuben."

"There's water out there that I've never seen."

"Sal says the weather looks like it will hold for a while. It will be full sun and there'll be some good seas, moderate winds, five to seven knots in the afternoons."

"I was hoping for that."

"There's your boy down there now," Nelson said. He walked out from behind the counter and went to the window.

"It can't be."

"Must have come in last night. He's eager, that's for sure."

"Damn it, I'm not ready, Nelson." My hand began to tremble and I grabbed it with the other, steadied it, but powerless, I knew, to minister to the shuddering in my torso and other limbs. My emotional insurrection.

"There's nothing to do now, Reuben, but take to the sea," Nelson said. "It has something true about it that will deliver peril or pleasure. I don't believe that a liar can rest long upon it. You will have your answer."

As I got up from the table, he stroked his chin and looked hard down among the boats to Jonas. I followed his gaze. There was no joy to see the boy there. But a resolution was possible now; the truth was waiting for me. If I were to resurrect my life, I had to believe that. There was a fire burning inside me and it scorched all that I thought was good. And how I cried for sanctuary, for a full measure of hope and moral affirmation, for June's exoneration. I knew I betrayed her by that very suggestion, but there was nothing left but to see my treacherous ambition through now.

He stood on the dock. I could see how he looked about, for me perhaps, or seizing the moment to reacquaint himself with the world of boats. Then he turned to her, *my June*. I wanted to know his thoughts, his motives. I wanted to know what moved him, what secrets he kept. I wanted to know what darkness lived inside him, what he was capable of doing. There was something that he knew. There was no one else. It had to come from him.

I stood at the door to leave and Nelson turned to me. He seemed to smile, but it wasn't that. His old eyes wanted to say something to me, something that would make all my worries go away. But he had no such power. He had his steadiness. All I needed to know was where he would be. He would be right there.

"Whatever happens, Reuben," he said, "you'll handle it."

"Yes." I nodded, but I wasn't so sure.

Closing the door behind me, I stepped out into the sun. Nelson had raised the flags for another season, the Canadian and American. They moved in slow soundless folds against the blue sky. I didn't want to look away from them. Something infinite there mesmerized me, that unimaginable space. Still, I knew I couldn't remain in its spell for long, and started down the dock.

Sea Chronicles 1

JONAS TURNED AWAY FROM the boat as he saw me coming down the dock. Slowly he raised his arm to wave to me. A boy not yet a man with something to tell me. In spite of my resistance, the space between us was closing. He was still far away, and there was only the shape of him, his youth that was expressed in his posture and the round and faultless shape of his face. Then the sound of my footfall on the weathered wood and sea sounds, the incessant consternation of gulls, the gurgle of motors idling, and dying voices flung out over the flat water. I could feel the strain in me, the grim bite of my mouth and fear damming my throat. And then those eyes that would reveal what was authentic and true, or perhaps a ruse to deceive me, those soft eyes, those fetching eyes that could not be forgotten.

"Mr. Dale," he said, "what a day. Can you believe it?" An unfamiliar smile.

It startled me, his even teeth and enthusiasm. "Yes," I agreed, "great sailing weather." I realized just then that I had to reel in my preconceptions, my judgements, and be aware of what a bright boy could read in my face like a book of intentions. We stood there a moment as if waiting for our next lines in a script. I could see that he looked to me. "So, Jonas, were the books helpful?" His name, a soft and sleepy exhalation still bitter on my lips.

"Oh, yeah," he said eagerly — his cue now. "I read them everyday, over and over. I loved it. It wasn't like studying in school. That was okay, but this was different somehow. It was fun. There's so much to learn. There's so much to know. It blew me away. Like tacking. 'The further a boat sails from a line directly downwind of the objective, the more likely it is to be adversely affected by a wind shift. And when a tide is running across the wind on the lee bow, an advantage can be gained because it increases the speed of the wind and alters its direction . . .'"

"That's impressive," I said. "You memorized every word."

"I think I can plot a course. Charts are so cool."

"They're important, and not so simple."

"I know they are," he said. "I practised."

"We can go over the charts for the strait."

"I already know them. I studied them. I know all the tides and buoy positions from here to Campbell River."

I watched him when he looked away, the same way that he watched me. He was anxious to sail, that I could see, and I detected a subtle insolence and defensiveness in his voice and attitude. But he was still not yet a man; the young can't be told, I remembered. Then something began to impose itself upon my will, random thoughts that weren't so unexpected. The thought that he had touched June worked like a screw in my brain, standing there so close to him. I could feel my hands. They wanted him, to get it all out right then and there, shake him senseless, take him by the throat and squeeze it out, like toothpaste, until those seductive eyes popped out of his head, and he set her free. I fought against it, struggled to find my skilled and artful will — that mature and experienced part of me Nelson spoke about. Oh, I bastardized it, I was sure, but it served me now. It had to if I were to succeed.

"So, we should get started," I said, regaining my composure. "Are you staying at the motel?"

"Yeah, I guess so. I was hoping that I could stay on board."

He caught me off guard. "Not now," I said. "We'll take it one day at a time." He was disappointed, so glum all at once.

"When are we going to sail?" He stood staring down into *my June*.

"Let's go over the program," I said, searching now for the things that I would impress upon him, a measured formality. "Sailing is an exhilarating but serious venture. We need to be prepared. Today we'll take inventory of all the elements on the boat. We'll go over every function, every purpose, from the radio to the bilge. We start with a sound ship. The equipment is paramount. Safety depends on it. All has to be in working order. Nothing can be overlooked. We need fresh water. The head has to be inspected, propane for the galley stove. The battery needs to be checked, safety gear requires inspection and survival suits stowed properly. Nothing can be missed.

"And there on the deck, well, that's where sailing comes alive, the winches and stays and shrouds, the spreader and the boom." I went aboard and unlocked the cabin, then turned to him. "And we'll have to fit the sails, the mainsail and headsail. So we can't get ahead of ourselves. We'll take her out tomorrow under power so you can get the feel of it. Not too far. Halfmoon Bay will be a good start."

"Can I steer?" he asked, leaping over the details and his eyes lighting up again.

"Yes, you can steer," I said to assuage him. He was a sensitive boy and I knew now that I would do well to accommodate him. "Come aboard," I said. "Go over the charts that we'll need for tomorrow. They're on the navigation table."

"I know where they are."

"I know you do, Jonas." I said turning to leave. "I'll be back with the sails. You can help me rig the sheets to the clew." I started up the dock and didn't get far before he called out to me.

"Mr. Dale."

I stopped and turned to him. I waited, alert, mindful of the ambivalent space between us.

"Thanks for doing this," he said. "You don't know what this means to me."

I stood a moment, looking at a boy, his long elegant neck and the boneless slack in his arms. A breeze rushed by my cheek whispering soft sounds in my ear. All about me were people chattering and cheerful coming down to their berths. I noticed that they wore white. It seemed the sailor's choice. They were illumined among the brilliant boats where the sun gleamed, solar paint awash on the hulls and decks. There was something timeless just then, an all-rightness that a warm spring day can press upon you. Could I be just a teacher, showing him how a bow slices through the green sea, listening for the pop in the mainsail — a reduction to the essential act of sailing? He watched me from the cockpit, waiting for a response. He seemed so harmless. Because I couldn't tell him the truth, I smiled at him, and continued up the dock.

Sea Chronicles 2

~⌢~

WITH THE MAINSAIL secured on the boom and the headsail rolled and tied to the lifelines along the foredeck, *my June* was ready for the open sea. I will admit that I was sour in my stomach as I called out to Jonas to push off the bow. Oh, we had studied the charts, a rudimentary plot of his I praised for the good of the day that promised calm seas, well suited for the diesel engine. I knew the water well enough, but never on my own, now the skipper and the mate. It was all I could do to fasten the sails right side up, and still there would be proof of that when the time came and we hoisted them like mariners or morons before a favourable wind.

"The stern rope, Jonas," I directed now, "and watch yourself over the rails."

He was nimble on his feet. "Aye, aye, captain," he said playful in his excitement at taking up the line and tossing it aboard then following behind.

"Pull the fenders, Jonas, and keep watch on the foredeck . . . Ease yourself along the cabin. Use the grab-rail now. A good eye until we get clear of the marina." He was spirited in his role as student and went about his tasks effortlessly. I could see that he had studied well and paid attention to my coaching. He looked the part in his sneakers and water-proof sailing suit. We were twins in our yellow outfits. I had no choice but to bring June's down for him although it troubled me to see him in it. Never mind, I had to push on; it was all routine now in the sailing world, with a crew setting out for the day.

The boats were tight together and he called out like a pirate as a sloop shoved away from its berth. "Avast, Captain, a ship off the starboard bow, a Spaniard ship by the looks of her. Arr, it'll be heavy with gold doubloons, I'd say. And there to port, sir, it's the galleon of that dreaded Jack Sparrow and his renegades. They have a mind for our booty, sir. Pillaging the coastal waters, their business. All muskets and cutlass, Captain. And there's an idle ship there, like an island it is, never seen the likes of her. The King's ship, no doubt, the finest to sail the seven seas. Paid for by the commoners. All clear now, Captain, the sea awaits us."

It was an unusual departure. I smiled at his wit, his keen articulation, his language that drew a laugh inside me that I would not disclose. And how amused I was when he identified Dr. Bender's yacht as the King's ship. A disarming moment that both confused and entertained me. I looked back to the marina with lucent gulls wheeling in our wake and crows that would not venture further. Their raucous shouts seemed a declaration of my madness, my clandestine scheme. Farewell fool. Then an unmoving figure standing on the peripheral dock. It was Nelson. I knew his shape and where he would be. He did not wave. It was so much like him to be there, just watching *my June* clear the breakwater.

Jonas returned to the cockpit, anxious to take the wheel. There was a slight ripple on the water and clear sailing before us. Conditions were good. "Here," I said, "take the wheel, Jonas. There'll be a few boats cruis-ing to Halfmoon Bay. They should be coming up our port side and you'll need to give way. Watch your compass here. Stay on a course of 10 de-grees. Look at the wake behind us and watch for drift. There'll be a group of small islands on your starboard bow. Be watchful of logs. A sailboat under power doesn't respond well to an abrupt course correction. So have a far-seeing eye now."

He took hold of the wheel like a proper sailor, standing tall with his eyes keen through the mast and rigging and sweeping across the horizon. *my June* seemed lifeless with her naked spars. Although the diesel engine under him made slow gains, he didn't seem to mind. He was at the helm, out on the Salish Sea, rapt with the mysteries of life. I stepped away and left him to his watch. Looking out across the strait, I felt the blue-green ocean sizzling against the hull. I always sensed the hunger of deep water, an unseen world cold and unknown to me. Shafts of green light driven down through the kelp forests to the rich bottom life of gaudy dimness. Now there was only that argent wrinkle of reflected light tossing around human endeavour. I never felt settled on the water, never felt moved to tranquil reflection. I was always on edge, uneasy to be caught floating in such dark complexion, ever-shifting and indifferent to my competency.

Nonetheless, there we were running up the coast at four knots with Jonas at the wheel, and the only thing on his mind it seemed was the bearing on the compass. There was a constant look of satisfaction on his face, a noble smirk of pride. He seemed to be born to it. Some people seem so fearless when they set out. Too fearless perhaps, in Jonas's case, because I was sure he was not noticing the power cruiser coming up fast in our wake.

It was long and lean and ripped the surface at better than forty knots. It seemed something boring out of another world, so suddenly it appeared upon us. The savage grind of its engines screamed at us to give way. Then it turned abruptly to our port quarter. Jonas saw it then, but I could not find the words for him, instructions from the teacher, a course of action to avoid the imminent wash. All at once it was alongside and gone, two men waving to us. I wondered if the broad sea had too much emptiness for them, or perhaps it was just a thoughtless act, taunting the vulnerable for some boorish pleasure.

The wash was on its way, displacement waves like a force-five wind that would hit us broadside and flood the deck. I was unsure just then, tentative, seized by inaction until Jonas called out to me, sharp crackling orders, his jarring command.

"Close the companionway!" he shouted.

I moved at once and locked the shutters. I could feel the boat shifting to port, then lifting as the first wave topped the deck and slapped the back of my knees. Seawater sloshed about and drained away. The waves dissipated quickly and went on to the distant shores and all calm returned. A moment gone without witness or redress. And there he was, bringing the wheel around.

"I tried to take the waves at forty-five degrees," he said. "I must have read it in one of the books."

"You knew what to do," I said. I watched him, his confidence. My bruised ego stuffed away.

"What's with that?" he said, replaying it now.

"Some people just don't have a clue."

"That was a freakin' water rocket!"

"There was no need to come up on us like that," I agreed.

"Crazy asses."

"You did well, Jonas."

"That was bad," he said with a laugh in his throat. "Let's do it again!"

He couldn't stop talking about it. We passed Trail Islands moving toward Halfmoon Bay. He paid little attention to the sea lions basking on the rocks. An eagle gaffed a bright fish alongside us and he ignored it. It was danger that excited him. I was glad that it was over, that the cabin was not flooded. I was also stuck in disappointment, my own inability to respond in a moment of crisis. Oh, the captain's discontent. I brooded while he recounted his glory to the disregard of the living sea.

As we cruised alongside Welcome Beach at the entrance to Halfmoon Bay, Jonas remained at the wheel. I came up beside him, wary of the many boats nearby and the changing depth below us. I pointed to a suitable anchorage offshore from the beach. He pulled back the engine throttle, handling it well, knowing when to make his course adjustments around rafts of kelp. He was a natural sailor. I suppose it was the temperament of his youth that was aroused by near misadventure. That time in our lives when the future was just too far away, and our mortality farther still.

I directed Jonas to drop the anchor from the bow. I could feel it bite into the seabed. The line tightened, and *my June* was secure. I watched him, always my covert vigilance. He was quiet now, having fallen from his euphoria. The forests were close, and all around us a rough green texture, unbroken, a grand painting of a mountain. I could feel its presence against the lasting sensation of the sea. Then I noticed that he looked toward the beach, to a couple walking along. They stopped to kneel now and then, beachcombing, picking up small things, bits of glass. Treasures, I knew. It broke my heart to see them, to know that I could no longer do that simple thing. June and her pocketful of shells and stones.

And how odd for Jonas to recognize this. He returned along the cabin to the cockpit. He wanted to say something. He had his head down. I wondered what it could possibly be.

"Did you do that?" he asked. His eyes avoided me, moved about fitfully.

"Beachcombing?"

"Yeah, looking for stuff."

"One of our favourite things to do," I said.

He just nodded, a firm pressing of his lips. It seemed he wanted my memory, a surrogate experience perhaps.

"I'll go get lunch," I said. I left him there with his motives.

Down in the galley I was relieved to be alone for a few minutes. I went to the fridge and removed the sandwiches I had prepared at home. Sailing lessons came with a complimentary lunch. There was something preposterous about the whole affair, I was thinking, not to mention June as if she were out of bounds, forbidden. Jonas was her student and I her husband, a common association. How was I going to resolve the clash of conjecture, root the truth from its burrow? How was I to listen if the talk between us was crippled with common chatter?

I returned to the deck with a plate of sandwiches and granola bars. "Hope you like egg salad," I said.

"Sure," he said. His hands reached hungrily.

We sat on the cockpit benches in the noon sun eating our sandwiches. The bay was a panorama of boats and sea ducks, and the rising mountains a wilderness when the eyes, strained from squinting, left the shimmering water for relief.

"We were here a few summers ago," I said. "We drove up one day, walked along Welcome Beach just as that couple were doing. Mrs. Dale liked to collect moon snail shells. She was always finding something to take home."

Jonas was looking over at the beach. Several couples now. He was not so talkative, more hungry than anything. Then like a fisherman who sees the rising trout, I tossed him a fly.

"On that day we found a coconut washed up," I said. "It was covered with barnacles. I was so excited. I imagined that it had made its way to us from some tropical island. Maybe it took years to travel that far. Mrs. Dale made a story about it, the journey of the coconut. Around the world it floated, through the endless calm and every rage of the sea, even in the bellies of whales. It washed up on remote beaches where half-naked children played with it before leaving it to an outgoing tide. It touched every shore of every continent. Finally it arrived here. It chose us. Currents and tides and serendipity."

He looked at me, that one eye closed to the sun like a boy. "That's not how it ends," he said.

"You've heard this story?"

"Yeah."

"Then finish it."

"It was a lot longer when Mrs. Dale told it. All the places that coconut went. At the end of the story she said, 'it could be, after all, that some guy from Nanaimo bought it at Safeway, then accidentally dropped it off his boat.'" That brightened his mood.

But that last line was something *I* had said, right there on the beach. It was the artful fusion of our creativity, the soaring heights of imaginative play, and then the plunging into laughter. It belonged to us. That thief before me, all innocence it would seem. Damn him and the corrupted weave of my life.

"She told you a lot," I said trying not to sound indignant. The patience of an angler.

"About what?"

"Our family."

"No. Mostly about sailing. Just stories."

"She told stories about the coconut and *my June* but never mentioned me?"

"Uh, no."

"Mrs. Dale never mentioned our daughters, Lori and Mandy?"

"Why would she? It was school, man. She never talked about stuff like that."

"Of course. Yes, you're right." I felt a fool all at once, having pushed too hard. I just wanted to say it. I wanted to ask him. Come out with it. *Did you have sex with my wife, you fucking little puke?*

I sat with the fear of the damage I may have done. I was teaching him to sail, giving him an opportunity to be out on the water, an experience that he would take away. Perhaps inspire him. But it wasn't true. I sought no higher ground for him. It was too personal, an obsessive need driving me to know. He was wondering now, I was sure of it.

"Hey, I have this ego," I said, jokingly. "You know, I'm this revered sailor. I just thought she would have told the class about her other half. No big deal. Who cares?" Then I stood up and shocked myself. "I am the king of the world!" I shouted out across the water. The turning of heads on the beach and Jonas doubling over.

"Never expected that," he said.

"Time for a beer?"

"Yeah, sounds good."

"Just one, you're driving."

"You're okay, Mr. Dale."

"I have my moments. And it's Reuben."

There was nothing gained there at Halfmoon Bay, no answers. I learned dishonesty and the farthest reaches of deception. I realized that at the end of the day, like the journey of the coconut, Jonas could have been just some kid from Vancouver who found his way to me through the tides of providence, an innocent and blameless apprentice, student of the Salish Sea. But that temperamental boy was reaffirmed when we were leaving the bay to return to Seaside. That same power cruiser passed in front of us in the distance, the same speeding profile. Jonas raised his hand and took aim. He tracked them with a cold patience. Then his hand jerked up twice as the bullets in his head took them down. And then something came out of his throat: the laugh that Nelson likely heard when the candles flickered and snow fell thick on Main Street.

Sea Chronicles 3

The weather was about to change. Nelson came down to the boat scratching his head and eyeing me sceptically. "There's one day of sailing out there, Reuben," he said. "Sal says that a low-pressure system is sneaking down. It will hit Comox in the afternoon. There'll be good winds, but the skirts might give you trouble. Then near gale winds or stronger. Same for the rest of the week. So stay south of Thormanby Island. You'll have a few hours. Looks like this is it."

The engine was running. Jonas was in the galley stowing our supplies for the day, but he heard Nelson's news plain enough. He rushed out of the cabin.

"We're still going out?" he said.

"Just long enough to raise the sails," I told him.

"That's it?"

"You need to pay attention," Nelson said. "The weather has no favourites."

"What does that mean?" he said, surly now. He didn't like Nelson.

"Jonas, we'll go out, just like we planned," I said to reassure him. "We just can't get caught out there."

"You said that you would teach me how to sail. You promised."

"I offered to teach you. But I have no control over the weather."

"This is bullshit!"

"Hey, I'm close to shutting this ship down," I said angrily. "This is your last opportunity. You better think about it, Jonas. I don't need to do this!"

He stood there and fumed. It was quite remarkable, his swift muta-tion, once agreeable now defiant. Nelson was speechless. I could tell by the way he looked at me that he wanted me to end it right there. I tried to remember why I had asked Jonas to come back, a kid who had a tough life, the story of his father and mother's death in Sarajevo. My own capri-cious motives had no solid footing, a tangled affair that I had created from wild intimation. There was no resolution in mere reason. Still, I would heed Nelson Grommet and end it that day.

I took the wheel while Nelson untied our lines and pushed us off. He reserved any parting advice for me. I knew he could see my irritation. There was nothing that could be said to appease my displeasure. We would sail out into the strait; a few trips around the block then bring her back. Then I would bid Jonas farewell. He would take whatever he learned back with him, an experience, an inspired opportunity. It all didn't seem to matter now. He had nothing to tell me. I had nothing to ask him. He was a young man struggling with his past, as we all do. I could manage that one last day at least, and then I would toss the rem-nants of all things incomplete into the sea.

We left the marina under power. I made sure we were fitted with safety harnesses over our sailing jackets. It was unlikely we would need to use our lifelines, but I wouldn't take any chances with the weather. I looked back at Nelson who was walking up the dock. I suppose he just couldn't watch. The flags above the marina store were moving, extended now, a light breeze from the northwest. Jonas stood by the cabin. He was quiet, perhaps reflecting on the morning, his petulance. I knew when to leave someone alone, to let them work it out, whatever it was. Once we were outside the breakwater, the water sliding along the hull seemed to whisper to me, soothe me. There is a quality to the sea that wants to mend our broken parts, that enters us through our eyes and all of our senses.

The sun was bright, warm on my neck, and the time had come. Reducing speed, I brought *my June* into the wind. "Jonas, ready the sails now," I called out to him. "Untie the headsail then take the shock cord off the boom. Stand by the main halyard winch and prepare to raise the mainsail." All marine formality now.

I turned off the engine, left the wheel and joined Jonas on the cabin roof. He was grave in his work, with a dour mouth as he loosened the sails. After checking the mast track and the boom, I inserted the handle into the winch, put a turn on it and watched as the sail came up, right side up. If that was a good omen, I didn't know, but I could see how Jonas responded to the rising sail.

"Take her up by hand," I said to him. "Hoist the halyard until your arms burn and then I'll finish it with the winch."

Jonas seemed to like the work. The mainsail unfolded from the boom like a cloud, and he heaved until the luff of the sail began to catch the breeze. He stepped back as I finished the sail. He smiled now, as *my June* was all at once a sailing ship. I returned to the cockpit and eased her into a port tack with Thormanby Island on the lee shore. The weather seemed perfect for sailing, a blue sky full over the sea, with clouds gathering and stacking over the mountains. Everything had an amplified brilliance, as if looking through a polished lens where colours seemed richer and life seemed worth living.

"Standing by to raise the headsail, Reuben," Jonas said breaking out of his dissatisfaction.

The sound of my name softened me. Was he sorry? "Take the end once around the winch and hoist away, Jonas. Finish it with the winch but don't over-hoist. Watch the luff as you go."

As the headsail came up, the sea breeze caught it well. *my June* surged and heeled. With his mouth open, Jonas looked up through the sails, as if wondering about the nature of wind and shapes, what a man could do. The tack was true and would hold windward for a time.

"Take the wheel," I said. "Just stay the course. I'll help back off the headsail when we're ready for the starboard tack." Jonas took the wheel and I stood aside.

There he was sailing *my June* on his own. Perhaps it was a dream that had come true. It was possible that I had fulfilled what the best part of me wanted for him. His hair was blowing away from his face, a proper young sailor. I couldn't help thinking of that unfulfilled part of me. It was the idea, a glimpse of a forgotten longing, an image of my unsatisfied projection. How swiftly I forgot what the day was all about. Then on the starboard beam a line of tall black fins appeared.

"Killer whales," Jonas shouted, excited to see them coming fast — on a collision course it seemed. "They're going to hit us!"

They seemed to appear out of nothing, a pod of eight orcas, females and calves and a bull with a dorsal fin like a black sail. "Steady, Jonas," I said. "They'll pass under us."

They blew one by one, followed by sharp sucking gasps, the vapour of their breaths out behind them. As one glistening body, they all submerged, with the tip of the bull's fin still slicing the sea. They resurfaced, black and shimmering with their white throats. On they came as we watched. They were like ebony torpedoes about to take us midship, the water lifting and parting from their great glossy heads. The moment comes when you trust a wild thing, its ancient intelligence, and our utter inability to manoeuvre out of the way. And I did trust because I was nothing, we were nothing. They went under, deep and long, under *my June*, slipped down into their seamless world. The blur of white markings like traffic through a rain-streaked window. I went to the rail as they came up forward off the port beam heading up the gut of the strait.

"Let's follow them," Jonas said. He was a boy who had touched and felt his own wilderness in the sight of such power and beauty.

"We won't keep up with them, Jonas."

"Come on," he insisted.

"We need to change the tack," I said, agreeing now. It was part of our sailing itinerary and I could see no harm. They would be long gone. "Wait until I tell you to go hard to port. Steady on the wheel now."

I readied the headsail for the new tack and uncleated the working sheet, maintaining the tension and manning the winches. Soon the sheets were ready. I could see the whales were now blowing far out into the strait. "Starboard tack now, Jonas. Strong to port."

As Jonas brought the wheel around, *my June* followed. I released the old sheet so that the headsail filled and the mainsail boom swung. We heeled and bit into the sea in pursuit of the whales. We caught a surge of wind as it licked the tops of waves. The spray was whipping across our bow; we tasted salt and freedom. There comes that moment in sailing when there is nothing else in the world, so present are we to sensation and perhaps mortality, when awe enters the body and we are suddenly thrust into some profound understanding. I had forgotten that such a state existed. It was June who said to me on a similar day, when a grey whale had been reported off of Vancouver, with words that only she could find, *I am the macro and the micro and the harpooner of old Nantucket*. I laughed because I had no idea what she meant. It was a silly thing to say perhaps. But so many things went over me, emotive, abstract, when I did not allow myself to understand. It was always enough that she knew.

"They stopped!" Jonas trumpeted, so stimulated he was by the sight of them gathering there before us.

I could see the agitated waters, the wild splashing as an orca breached then slammed back onto its side, its white belly ephemeral in the sun. Then another joined in until the surface was an ebullition, with whales heaving their impossible weights clear and free of the sea. We gained on them. They seemed to be playing, teasing us to follow. *my June* was heeling well, the mainsail and headsail trimmed for speed. She closed the distance as the whales tossed and revelled like children in a pond.

Then I felt it, a cold slap against my chin, and there up through the rigging the pop of sailcloth taut in their sheets. The air about us was charged with the hem of the coming storm that Nelson had warned about. Beyond the irresistible diversion of whales, a pale yellow horizon tumbled while the many small islands were all but seized by the front rushing down the strait. I was alarmed. I stared into the cold reality of my limitations. I knew I wouldn't be able to manage the coming surge. I turned to Jonas now, the urgency concealed in a consoling hand on his shoulder.

"Time to turn back," I said.

"What, we've just got out here," he said jerking his head. That look of his scorching me.

"You can feel it, Jonas," I reasoned. "The temperature is dropping; Comox has disappeared. The storm is coming."

"The whales are right there. Come on!"

I had to think fast. The wind was picking up, whistling through the stays. "I'm calling in, Jonas," I said. "Just stay on course. Hold the wheel. It'll fight you windward." I glanced out over the water, the crowning waves. Lasqueti Island disappeared. I hurried to the cabin and picked up the radio.

my June — Seaside — over

Seaside — my June — over

Seaside, sailing northwest — location 8 kilometres west of Thormanby Island. Weather coming. Update Seaside — over

my June, Seaside broadcasting over the hour. Front south of Comox. Winds from northwest 20 knots. Advise return to Seaside, my June — over

Copy that, Seaside — over

What's your condition, my June? — over

Under sail, coming about — over

Wait your arrival, my June — Seaside out

Thanks, Sally — my June out

I closed the companionway and hatches and returned to the cockpit. All bright sun and blue sky above us, with Jonas defiant at the wheel. The whales had moved on, it seemed. I couldn't find them. We had gone too far. We were in the middle of the strait heading toward a gale. I clipped our lifelines to the stern rail. "We're turning back now," I announced as strong as I dared. "Ease her about."

"No, we can find them again. Stay the course."

"Give me the wheel, Jonas. This is not a game. The whales are gone!"

"This is nothing!"

I could see that queer side of him, how he turned toward what threatened him — danger, feeding something inside. "Step aside, Jonas, do it now!" I demanded. "You can't handle this. It's too much for you. We have to slow her down. You'll need to reef the mainsail!"

"You promised me. I know what I'm doing. I read all those books. You're just afraid!"

"Jonas, what's wrong with you?" The inflection of his words seemed to change, his face distorting. Another personality was emerging. It was a shocking transformation, a mutinous moment that was worse than I feared. It was what Nelson had tried to tell me all along.

"There's nothing wrong with me. Why don't you enjoy the ride?"

"Jonas, you're not making sense. You don't know what you're saying." I pleaded with him. I had to do something fast. It was a frightening moment to look into his feral eyes — nothing boyish there now. I wanted to get away from him, but I was imprisoned on that heeling deck. There was no more time.

I reached for the wheel and took it. I shouldered him, but his hands held fast like vises as we jostled on the tilting deck. Waves were coming over the bow and the dark troughs were deepening. We were in grave danger of turning over.

"Fuck off, old man!" he growled, shoving me back. "You're not taking this boat. I know her. She's mine. We'll sail right into the storm. She's done it before!"

It was a desperate eternity, windward still and ten-foot waves cresting with the tops blowing foam. I felt helpless, unable to find a way to take back the wheel. There was something alien and sinister rising in him. I had to find a way to turn him back. I could knock him senseless with a fist. It was a terrifying thought that I had to consider. I could send out a mayday call, ready the survival suits, but that time had passed. I had to reach him somehow and pull him out of his mania before the gale knocked us down.

Seawater ran from my cold scalp and dripped from my chin as I held onto the stern rails with bloodless hands. The sea heaved and the blue sky closed over us. There was no seasickness in me but a harrowing realization that I might not survive the day. As the water poured over the deck I had a sense that the solution could well be under my feet, upon the very thing of his obsession — *my June*, and the stories he had heard. I moved near him with one hand on the rail. The tension ran through me like a steel rod.

"Mrs. Dale told me about the storm," I said above the wind.

"Into the eye, full and by, all plain sail!" he called out to an imaginary crew.

"It was just a story, Jonas. It didn't happen. It wasn't real."

"Does this feel like it's real?"

"Jonas, please listen to me!"

"Are you afraid to die?"

"Is that what this is all about?"

"Can't you feel it?"

"She wouldn't want you to do this."

"She? I know what her name is."

"June would want you to turn back."

"You don't know her."

"She's dead, Jonas!"

He hesitated just then, as if reconciling the past and present, the sea lifting all around him and the strands of his hair wet against his cheeks like leeches.

"I called her June," he said turning to me, making sure I looked into his eyes. "Did you know that?"

"That's all right."

"She did mention you, you know. I lied. She said you're old and that you couldn't please her."

"What are you talking about?" There it was, but I didn't want it now.

"You're an old man," he said mocking me. "You're all used up. Look at you!"

"Shut your mouth!"

"She used to hold me. Did you know that? She cared. She cared about me. She wanted to help. No one else gave a shit about me at that school. But she did. And she loved *it*. You know what I'm talking about. You know, old man, don't you?"

"What did you say?" Our sopping faces just inches apart and my knuckles like hammers, never imagining that they would be bared on such a menacing sea.

"She said that you were boring. She was lonely, man. Do you know what that's like? Do you?"

"Shut up!"

"I made love to her!"

"Why do you want to do this to me? I've done nothing to you."

"I saw it in your face, that first day. You wanted me to go away. You hated me. Don't you remember? You're like everyone else. But she was different!"

"I don't hate you."

"You didn't deserve her. She didn't love you, old man. She loved me!"

"You better stop!" I didn't want to hear it and regretted every decency in me.

"We fucked in the classroom after everyone left for the day. Did you hear me?"

"You bastard. You're insane. That's not true!"

"It's true," he shrilled. "It's true. She's waiting for me. I want to be with her. She's out there now!" He reared his head back, an animal yawl against the storm escaping.

My hands were soon to be around his neck, a lifeless thing wrung like a rag. I could fight him to the death, kill him before he killed me. But there was another way. I could allow my own destruction. As if to finally reconcile that snowy morning when death brought her to me. I could turn away from every sad story. The sea seemed all at once a release. I could just roll over the side and it would be finished — four minutes in the cold Salish Sea. As if every moment in my life had accumulated, merged with the pounding waves that would kill me, my karmic debt paid in full. I had not imagined that the sailing lesson would be like that. But it had been my plan after all, to draw it out of him, to discover the truth. It seemed now that I was tied to him, Jonas, a boy without a last name. I was the unwitting accomplice to his death wish, the means and the end.

I could feel the tomb of a grey world about to receive us. The mainsail tore along the boom and quickly shredded. The cutting rain stung my face raw. The full force of the storm would soon be upon us. But it no longer mattered. Nothing mattered now. Then I felt the loom of something over my shoulder. I braced against the port rail. A dark presence reared above me as *my June* dropped into a deep ravine of sea. Before I could turn to face it, it fell upon us, a green tower of water crashing over the deck. In an instant Jonas was gone, as if he had never been there at all. The deck was awash and tilting dangerously.

I managed to reach the stern where his lifeline held him still. Oh, the terror in his eyes as he slipped below the foam and fury of the sea with every rise and fall of the deck. The great troughs of waves were drowning him. I took hold of his lifeline but I couldn't lift him. The weight of water tugged at him, held him down like Ahab tethered to his white whale. Once more the stern came up, and he came heaving forth with a great gasp of breath, only to be snatched down again. I waited for the next surge. I couldn't fail now. He wouldn't survive another plunge. The blurred shape of him with his flailing arms appeared, and then up he came. I reached for his harness with dead hands. Somehow my fingers found a hold and I heaved with all my strength. Over the stern and onto the deck Jonas spilled like a fish.

I helped him along the deck and set him down by the companionway, transferring his lifeline to the starboard rail. He was cold but alive. He drew his knees up, unable to raise his head.

By some reckoning of the world that I didn't understand, *my June* was slowly returned to me. Still we pitched perilously into the storm. I returned to the cockpit where the wheel was spinning wildly. I managed to stop it and held it steady; full into the waves, twenty-footers now. The bow heaved up and then fell away into deadly valleys black and dispassionate. Then the headsail ripped and the bow went under. All seemed lost, but *my June* fought on, the foaming deck rising once again, ascending like some undying thing, a white apparition on a savage sea. Jonas raised his head and looked to me, a question in his sad eyes.

"Hold on!" I called out to him.

I could see the crush of his life through the spray and the brine, a boy broken in a desolate dream. The sea rose and fell and I slowly brought her about, measured now between undulating mountains of rioting waves. Soon the wind met us starboard and then on our heels, waves washing over the stern and down our necks, never giving a moment's reprieve, still in a mood to wash us both away. It chased us into the afternoon, licking at us with punishing tongues, pounded the deck and shook the spar and rigging with a deafening might.

There was nothing to do but try to bring her home. The wind pushed us leeward, but I managed to find the breakwater, with the sea smashing the granite barrier with maddening fists. I turned on the little motor. With the headsail ruined, I fought for the narrow neck of protected waters. Jonas was silent, not a word from him. To hate him or pity him, it seemed that I had my answer. There was only a dead emptiness inside me, gutted of all feeling, flensed of any cleverness or pretence I might have had.

Nelson was standing at the end of the dock in his dripping green slicker. He raised a hand and held it there as if saluting our return. I knew he had feared a ghost ship floundering somewhere out in the grey upheaval, but there we were, coming in with ragged sails. And land and trees and Seaside's rising streets.

The Last Hero

THE NEXT MORNING I awoke to knocking at the door. I couldn't get out of bed. Such heaviness visited me, my body held down like Gulliver's. I existed in a dreamy space where sounds entered dreams, became part of them, shaped fantastic scenes that could not be separated from reality. Then I remembered the sea. It writhed inside me still. It was no dream. I had been close to death, but I hadn't been afraid to die. After we had left the dock, and Jonas had climbed into his car with his pale good looks bleached from him, I was angry, but I also I felt a sense of sorrow for him. I never made him wrong or evil. I did not want to harm him. And I never blamed him. What would be the point? He had touched my wife, destroyed every moment that I ever had with her. But she was dead and I couldn't get her back. I couldn't get her back to ask her why she had *touched* him — the greatest betrayal. I left Jonas to his own devices and a firm suggestion never to return to Seaside.

When the knocking continued, I ignored it. Then came tapping at the bedroom window. I could see a face through the thin shears. That old woolly head. I stirred and he called my name.

"Reuben, it's Nelson," he said with his face up to the pane. "I'm not leaving until you get up."

I went to the window and pulled open the curtain. There he was cupping his eyes. He reared back when he saw my blushing nakedness. "Go away," I said.

"I'll be waiting in my truck," he said through the glass.

I slid open the window. "What are you doing, Nelson?"

"You need to come down for coffee, Reuben."

"I do?"

"I've come to get you."

"I suppose if I told you I don't want a cup of coffee, you still wouldn't go away?"

"You suppose right, Reuben. Get dressed."

I knew I wasn't going to win with Nelson. I dressed and left the house unshaven and got into his truck. He sat looking at me. I looked back at him. "I didn't think this old boat-puller ever left the marina," I said.

"Well, you might think that a 1967 Ford would be all used up. It's got rust, that's for sure. That's on account of living on the west coast. But she's only got 50,000 miles on her. Original clutch."

"Now I'm really glad you got me out of bed."

"Not a problem, Reuben."

We drove down the streets and I noticed rhododendrons and azaleas red and pink in the fervent gardens, the grounded sense of things, nothing fluid threatening to wash over the hood. I was glad to be on solid ground. Down at the marina I sat at my table, as if I owned it, claimed it that day when the colour appealed to me — that hopeful blue. But I wasn't feeling hopeful. I felt like the infirm out on a day trip. A flat-screen television hung on the wall.

I looked up to see *my June* in her berth. The remains of the sails had been removed. Nelson brought my coffee, with the orcas now scratched and fading.

"We followed them out into the strait," I said. "The way their dorsal fins sliced through the water ahead of us. It was something. I should have known better."

Nelson allowed my regrets to settle for a moment. "That was a fine bit of sailing, Reuben," he said. "The weather forecast changed."

"I couldn't get to the radio."

"Sally figured that much. She called off the Coast Guard when you appeared beyond the breakwater."

"Sails are ruined."

"I took them down."

"Thanks."

"Well, I'll be down at the fuel dock, Reuben, if you need me. One of these days I'll show you how to work the till. I'm going to add a few more tables along the window. Going after the lucrative coffee-drinker market."

"You'll have to ask more than a dollar."

"I was thinking a buck and a quarter. And they can watch the Blue Jays up there." He pointed to his new addition.

"I wondered how you got so rich," I teased. I managed to find humour lifting from my despair. Perhaps it was a device of my survival. And strangely, I couldn't tell him the details of his suspicions. I just couldn't. He knew what I was going through.

That's the way it was for a while. Every morning Nelson would knock on the door to get me out of bed. I would climb into his rusty low-miler and he would drive me down to the marina, where a cup of coffee and one of Sally's blueberry muffins would await me. He would tell me a thing or two, a new knot he had discovered, complete with a demonstration. Sometimes he would tell me the time of the next high tide or what bright star to look for in the night sky. But he never preached to me, never judged me for my foolishness. He never once drew a conclusion or offered an opinion about my ordeal. He knew that it was something big — more than he could sort out. He just wanted me to know that I was not alone, that he and Sally cared. I was their adopted son, it seemed to me, although I was only ten years younger than they were. He showed me how simplicity could free the mind of its troubles.

"Look at that," he would say for the umpteenth time, "how the cormorants sit on the pilings to dry their wings in the sun."

I didn't mind. I knew that Nelson drew some pleasure from the fact that they chose his marina. Eventually he taught me how to work the till, the cash and debit and credit cards. I made a sale or two, awkward and dumb when I forgot how to count. My new career was slow out of the gate, but it kept me occupied, kept me from thinking too much.

On the last day that Nelson came for me, I was waiting out in the driveway. The sun was moving in and out of the clouds but warm enough for shirt sleeves.

"You think you can make it for coffee on your own now?" he said to me in the truck.

"I think so," I said grudgingly. He would have kept coming for me, had I asked him.

"I never made it all the way up that mountain," I confessed to him.

"I was wondering about that."

"Just couldn't do it that day."

"There's always a second chance, Reuben. One day after closing I'll take you up there. No worries."

There was a good breeze and the flags billowed against their cords as I followed Nelson into the marina store. There was someone sitting at my table and she was holding a whale in her hands. She smiled. It was Shirley Plath-Mellencamp, home from Africa. She was wearing khaki shorts and her long legs were tangled under the table. I wasn't sure what to do. It was my table. I never shared it with anyone but Nelson. I thought that perhaps I would sit at one of the new tables. Would that be rude? So I stood uncomfortably and waited for Nelson. He would likely say something, I surmised, some clue to help me. Instead, he disappeared into the back and returned with a cup of coffee and set it down on my table. Then he looked at me whimsically.

"Just sayin', Reuben," he said. Then he turned away and left on his rounds.

I sat down. There we were face to face once again. "You came back," I said brilliantly.

"Hello, Reuben," she said, "and you're so right about Nelson Grommet, he seems to know what a person needs."

"Yes, he's a funny guy," I said. "I can't imagine my world without him."

"That says a lot about him. And you."

"I never had a friend like that." I realized just then what Nelson had done. It seemed that he did know what I needed. She was sitting right there.

We both turned to the window to watch him among the boats. I wondered what made him that way, to allow life to move through him. Shirley seemed to understand him. She told me about Somalia, the drought, the boy soldiers and the girls raped and the schools where her own children tried to bring them back to their innocence. Africa seemed lost in her narrative, too damaged to heal, an unapproachable hopelessness. She had gone to counsel a son and daughter and others in the camps. She had wondered if she could remain to do the good work, the desperate and loving work. Perhaps at another time but now she had to return. Her own wounds, it seemed, had followed her there.

As we shared the table with the sun streaming through the window, the story of Jonas and June crept out of me, shyly at first, and then on it came because it seemed safe to do so. A moment of hesitation was met by her sincerity; her depth of compassion was both astonishing and frightening. Knowing what she had seen, I realized my story seemed light fare. But she said to me, "We need not compare our pain. Pain is pain. It needs our attention. We do the best we can to lessen it in the world. And to heal it where we can."

When we had finished our coffee, Shirley pushed back her chair. "I would like to sit in the sun," she said. She got up and went to the door and out into the bright day. I followed her.

There were stairs from the promenade down to the beach. We sat on a log, resting our elbows on our knees and looking out over the Salish Sea. A thousand things for the eye and all the senses throbbing against the rank drift of the tide. There was comfort in her companionable presence, with scarcely a word between us. It did not seem necessary somehow, as if words were intrusions upon the order of the beach. So we sat and watched the movement of water, the sounds of waves, all the sounds of the sea. There were no boundaries with all things flowing together. It seemed just then that we were part of it all. Then she stood up all at once and stretched her legs.

"Sometimes," she said, "I forget the difference between loneliness and being alone." She rested her eyes on me for a moment, smiled, and walked away.

I watched her go, her long strides up the beach to the stairs, her hair swinging across her straight back. She was like water; she belonged to no one. Then she stopped and turned back to me.

"I live up there," she called out, pointing to a steep stairway that led to the townhouses above the promenade.

I stood and waved to her. "Are you going to stay?" But she only waved back. Her hand seemed to float in the space of the question.

I watched her reach the top and disappear. She seemed to linger there, something of her remaining. After a few moments I turned away from the mystery that was Shirley and went down to the water's edge and picked up a handful of stones and tossed them listlessly, one by one, into the sea, watching the rings, seeing how they touched, merged, and moved on. I remained there with the measured rhythm of the waves, their dissolving splash. Sea lettuce shredded and strewn. But I wasn't interested in the life at my feet or the sun scattering over the water. I thought about her words, obscure and unreachable. I didn't understand. Then I felt a deep sense of abandonment, like the stranded logs behind me and the long dead gull all white bone and wing. Perhaps loneliness was as fatal.

J Walking

∽

I CHECKED MY TELEPHONE messages when I got home.

Hello, Dad. This is Lori. How are you? Give me a call.

Hi, Dad. Mandy. I'm bringing a friend when we come out. Just thought I would let you know.

Reuben, it's Judy. Please call me.

I stared at the telephone, glad to hear from the girls, and that Mandy was bringing a boyfriend. But my feeling of comfort knowing that the girls would be coming was marred by the last message, the sound of the woman's voice. Judy. I had forgotten the message that I had left after finding a telephone number in June's purse. Her voice, devoid of social greeting, invoked a subtle demand. I called her.

"Hello."

"Judy, it's Reuben."

"Reuben, I got your message. I'm sorry I didn't call you sooner."

"Yes, I was looking for someone. When I called, I thought it was his number."

"Jonas."

"Yes," I said, surprise obvious in my voice.

"I know him."

"How do you know him?" I asked suspiciously.

"I taught with June. I was at her funeral."

"You're a teacher?"

"Yes."

"Right, I remember now. I spoke to you after the service. So how can I help you, Judy?" I asked, trying not to sound alarmed.

"We need to talk."

"About what?"

"Jonas and . . ."

"Jonas and *June*," I threw out aggressively.

"Yes."

This was what I feared. "I know something about that," I said.

"We need to talk, Reuben. Can you come to Vancouver?"

The abrupt question took me by surprise. "When?"

"As soon as possible."

This was sounding serious, I thought. "I suppose so," I agreed hesitantly.

"Can you get to Horseshoe Bay?"

"Yes."

"There's a coffee shop there, in the village. It's called The Bay Café on Bruce Street. Can you come tomorrow? Say at eleven?"

"I'll be there," I said, my voice sinking.

When I put the telephone down, I felt ill. I had no idea that it would be the worst of calls. I went into the living room to sit in my chair and stare into the landscape of my life. June's repellent indiscretion had sullied the life I thought we had together. What could come of a meeting with Judy? She sounded so businesslike and urgent. I supposed I had heard the worst of it on the roiling sea, *his* merciless and cruel confession. It was time to put it all in some place, a neat little box that was known only to me, sealed, where I could live with its story. Ahab was dead and I would put him back on the shelf.

In the morning I checked my watch as I backed the Subaru out of the garage. I would catch the Langdale ferry at 9:20. There were raindrops on the windshield, clouds rolling in uncoupled from the ocean, and random beams of sunlight splashing here and there. Unsettled weather, they called it, but a warm day. As I drove up Dory Avenue toward the Sunshine Coast Highway, I passed Bert and Rollie once again picking up their dogs' turds from someone's front lawn. Plastic bags of shit swinging in their hands. I waved enthusiastically because they wondered, I knew, what I was up to. They never seemed to have gotten over my splendid moment staring down Councillor Porter that day. I was forever elevated in their eyes. I admit that I was tempted to milk it whenever the opportunity to retell the story arose.

Because the road was wet, I slowed on the curves, paying attention to the sun filtering through the firs and cedars, a moment's blindness in the sudden light, then shadow. As usual, the ocean views and the mountains still covered with snow on the high peaks looked like a glossy page out of a tourist's guide. I passed through Robert's Creek and gave ample room to the bottle- and can-collectors working the ditches along the highway. I imagined the empties tossed from passing cars in the late night. The men depended on such thoughtless acts. Then my thoughts returned to the meeting that awaited me, what Judy would say, what I would say — always the mind in preparation, as if it could not tolerate surprises. I wondered what Nelson would do. I suppose he would just show up without a plan and trust that he would know what to say, what to ask. That simplicity. I didn't know why I couldn't do that. Why was it so hard? I had always given a problem my anxious speculation, trying to fashion a future that hadn't arrived. In the end, June would have solved it anyway. So now it seemed a reasonable thing to do, to trust myself and enjoy the drive, this once.

Gibsons was charming in the full sun, with Metro Vancouver shimmering in the distance past Bowen Island. I continued on, leaving my car in the parking lot in Langdale, and buying a foot-passenger ticket at the booth. After a short wait, I boarded the ferry and followed my fellow passengers up the stairs to the upper decks. Once the ferry had pulled away from its berth, I stood outside against the deck railing and looked out to the islands and mountains rising green from the water. I tried to remain present, to keep the coming meeting away, for a little while at least. But then I remembered June. How could I not? She would hug my arm when the breezes chilled her. As if she never wanted to let go. It was me of course, who never wanted her to let go. But even that memory was stained now, a smudge on a favourite photograph. Memories could no longer be trusted.

Once the ferry docked at Horseshoe Bay, I disembarked and walked out onto the asphalt. Passing a thousand waiting cars, I felt disoriented in the heat of the day. Then the village appeared beyond the acres of blacktop. Normally it had a lazy small-town feel. People would be walking unhurried in front of old houses crowded around aging but quaint shops and galleries. But I was only partially aware today, part of a crowd of people in movement. On Bruce Street I spotted The Bay Café. A woman sitting at a table on the patio watched me coming up the street and cross the intersection to the café. It was Judy. All at once I could feel a tightness in my chest, my body's rejection of simplicity and trust. The meeting had already begun.

She stood up and offered me her hand. "Reuben, thanks for coming. Did you have a good trip down?"

"Yes, it was good," I said, my voice quavering now.

"I already bought a coffee. I wasn't sure what you wanted."

"I'll go get one," I said.

I went into the café, bought my coffee, and took it to a counter to add cream and sugar. I was nervous, my hands trembling. I was afraid of what she would tell me, something more than I already knew. I dropped a brown sugar packet into my cup and burnt my fingers fishing it out. Then I slopped my coffee on the counter. A mess of sugar and puddles of coffee and cream. I stopped and took a long breath, wiped the counter with a napkin and hoped no one was watching. KLUTZ VISITS HORSE-SHOE BAY.

I managed to return to the table without leaving a trail and sat down. "So . . ."

"Well . . ." Nothing more.

We looked at one another awkwardly. It wasn't a good start. Judy was having difficulty, it appeared. She was a heavy woman who seemed uncomfortable in her body. She wore a cotton sleeveless blouse. There in the disappearing shade, perspiration was slick on her temples and neck. I wondered what was causing her distress. I waited for her to speak.

"I don't know where to begin," she said.

"Begin?"

"You see, I don't want to upset you."

"Just tell me whatever it is that you think I should know. Tell me about Jonas."

"All right, but first, let me ask you what you know of him."

"Well, he came to Seaside," I said. "He was an odd kid, kind of lost. He was taken with our boat, *my June*. He told me about his classes with June, how she helped him graduate. Things like that. He wanted to sail. So I made an offer to teach him. And it didn't go well. He told me things. Outrageous things. He seemed to be damaged somehow. Perhaps it was because he lost his father and mother at such a young age. They were murdered in Sarajevo. I don't know. But he is not a person I ever want to see again." I ended it there. I saw no need just then to reveal the details of that day of the storm.

"What kind of things did he tell you?"

I felt uncomfortable now. "If you have something to tell me, please tell me."

"This is very difficult, Reuben."

"Look, Judy, you asked me to come here," I said leaning over the table. I was growing impatient with her unwillingness to tell me what she knew. It seemed dependent on what *I* knew, what I was willing to say.

"Tell me what Jonas said."

It was clear now that she wasn't going to tell me anything more. And I was becoming unhinged there in the sun without knowing the truth. I finally had to give in to her. "All right," I said. "He told me that they had some kind of an affair. He said that he *fucked* her. Is that what you wanted to hear?"

"Oh, my goodness!" she said, shocked by my outburst. She looked around the patio, to others coming and going. "Reuben, I'm sorry," she continued, whispering to counter me. "I didn't want to upset you if I didn't have to. June didn't want you to know."

"It's true then?"

"I never thought you would find out. Then I got your voice message. Reuben is not a common name. I knew what you had discovered. I had to tell you the truth."

"June had an affair with a student."

"No, Reuben, no. June never did anything wrong. I worked with her. I knew her."

"You're going to have to explain. I don't understand."

"All right. Jonas made inappropriate advances toward June after class one day. At first she didn't tell anyone. She spurned him, made it clear that his behaviour was unacceptable. After that, she refused to help him after school. That upset him. She thought that he might be stalking her. She reported the incident to the school administration. He's not okay, Reuben. He needs help. You see, he filed a complaint with the school. He turned it around on her. He claimed that it was June who made the inappropriate advances. He threatened to press charges."

I felt a wave of relief, but still I was confused. "I found condoms in her purse."

She looked away all at once, the pulse of seconds, as if she wasn't expecting such news. Then she nodded after a time as an explanation returned to her. "June had a girl in one of her classes," she said, "whose parents didn't think to educate their daughter. There are a few out there. She was sexually active. She asked June to help her. So June gave her condoms to keep her safe. Some teachers get quite close to their students. They shouldn't interfere, but June wasn't the type to let anyone down, not an eighteen-year-old girl with her life in front of her."

"What did Jonas want?"

"I don't know. I suppose he wanted *her*."

"It must have been awful."

"Oh, the meetings, the questions put her through hell. She didn't want to retire; she was forced to, Reuben. She didn't want you to know. It cast such doubt. Accusations can change everything about a person, ruin reputations, careers. When you deny something, it somehow translates into a cover-up. Everyone is suspicious. The ministry has to act on complaints such as this. It happens. Some have crossed the line with their students, but it is extremely rare. Teachers are professional. It didn't matter to the school if June was innocent. It was all perception. June worried about police involvement, and that you would find out, so she took early retirement. Then she died."

"Oh, my God!" There in my chest a cavernous sob began to stir. Such release in her words, but not then. "Why wouldn't she tell me?"

"Because she couldn't."

"She was afraid that I wouldn't be able to handle it," I thought aloud.

"That wasn't it exactly, Reuben. I think she didn't want to see doubt in your eyes. She couldn't bear it. She had hoped it would be resolved."

"I was so blind. I should have been able to see. Everything seemed so normal."

"June was good at making things seem all right. But inside her . . ."

"The strain was too much. All this from a kid."

"We learned that he was with his mother when she was murdered."

"He never said that he was with her. He left that part out."

"They found him sitting beside her body covered in her blood. For two days he was with her. I read the reports in his school files when he first came to Royal Academy. There was always a certain compassion for him. The teachers gave him a break. He never talked about it. I suppose he had erased it somehow. And some of the kids picked on him. Teased him. He was very shy and kept to himself. I think there was some post-traumatic stress. There had to be."

I allowed the image of Jonas and his mother to recede in all its horror. "You knew June really well," I said.

"When you spend that much time with a person, more perhaps than your husband, you get to know them. I trusted her. I put my own career on the line supporting her. You know administrators. They don't like a fight, no controversy, nothing to draw attention. Private schools and their image — all prestige and integrity to uphold. They wanted to sweep it all away, and June with it."

"She would always ask me how my day was," I said. "I never really asked her how her day went. She rarely talked about her work. She was more interested in mine."

"June never did anything wrong, Reuben. It was Jonas. Believe me, she was innocent."

I sat and shook with my tears, as truth settled upon every blade of grass, every leaf and blossom, poured in an instant over the animate and inanimate. I had such love for June just then. I wanted to tell her so. I feared that I had not said it enough, that I did not touch her when she needed to be touched; that I did not listen to *her* story. I wanted her to know that I was sorry for doubting her. And through my bleary eyes I could see that Judy was relieved to be free of her burden. She wiped the sheen from her face with a towel that she carried with her, patted her neck and along her hairline. She had carried such knowing all that time — to spare me the anguish of June's ordeal. I was glad it was over.

She finished her coffee and stood up. The meeting was over. "It was nice seeing you again, Reuben," she said.

I stood and took her hand. "Thank you for telling me, Judy," I said. "I really appreciate what you tried to do for June. It means a lot to me."

"Closure," she said. "That's what they call it. And remember, we never had this conversation. I want to keep my job."

"No worries. But why did Jonas come to Seaside?"

"Something there, I suppose. Perhaps to be near her, or it could have been you, or the boat. I don't really know."

"What will happen to him?"

"He's just another sad story."

"Someone will help him?"

"Perhaps."

We stood there a moment with our impotence. And then our hands slipped free, and she walked away.

Tell it on
the Mountain

⸎

NELSON PICKED ME UP in his truck after he closed up the store, and
we set out for the Thunderbird Lookout parking lot. Because it was
early summer now, it would stay light until nearly ten o'clock. There
was time enough to climb the hill and have the sandwiches Sally made
for us, time enough to watch the last arc of the sun.

"Are you sure this thing can make it that far?" I said to him.

"Don't listen to him," he said, tapping the dashboard.

"I don't think it has ever been out of first gear."

"How's that?" he said shifting out on the highway.

"Impressive."

"You're in a pretty good mood," Nelson observed.

"Well, I guess I'm feeling all right," I said.

"It's a load off your mind."

"It has been quite a ride. I wasn't so sure I was going to make it."

"But you did, Reuben."

"I did. Now I just have to reach the top of that mountain."

"My dad used to say, *if you don't first succeed, suck eggs.*"

"Which means?"

"I'm not sure of the meaning, but I always liked the way he said it."

"Do you always wave your hands like that when you drive?"

"You know, Reuben, you're actually kind of funny."

"Really?"

"Well, not hilarious. But you have your moments."

"I always thought you were the funny one."

"No, not me. I can't tell a joke. And sometimes I just don't get it when a boater spins one for me down at the marina. I laugh anyway just in case. I always worry that I might laugh before the punch line. And what if it wasn't a joke at all, but something that happened to them that wasn't supposed to be funny? I get some strange looks."

"You see, now that's funny."

Nelson parked the truck, got out and shouldered his pack, then reached in the back for his walking stick. It had a sharp hook for a handle with a peculiar knot. A rich walnut finish.

"Thunderbird," he said to me as we started up the trail. "The head here." He held it up to me.

"It looks like a seagull," I said.

"Don't listen to him," he said to his walking stick.

The banter between us was easy now. I never had that kind of relationship with a man before. There had always been my hesitation, a wall that wouldn't allow such fellowship, a defensive measure to conceal Martin Rouse.

Going up the trail, I followed behind Nelson's long, solid strides into the shadows where the sun streamed down through the high limbs. I remembered the sounds of the thrush and winter wrens, and how they had frightened me — the lament of a solitude that I wasn't ready for. But now in the woods the thrush was silent. Trilling its high bubbling notes, the wren now seemed a good companion. The creek, as we neared it, was roaring with snow melt. Through trees I could see a white cascade driving down through the narrow gorge. The cool spray from the plunging creek felt soothing against my bare arms and face.

When the grade steepened, Nelson paused to rest, turning back to me and smiling. I looked at him above me — seventy-five years old in a few days — straight as a rod and hard as iron. He seemed undefeatable standing there. Then on he went until at last the trail cut across a wall of rock, and there it was, a promontory of grass and stone with wildflowers spilling out of the seepage. "Yellow monkey flowers," Nelson said. There was a rough cedar fence at the very edge of the lookout, with a dramatic view out over the strait, a world that seemed all at once redeemable under the chrome-red sun. Catching my breath, I felt a measure of accomplishment standing there. A warm wind rushed up the cliff beating the grass about us, as if alive in a tilted coppering landscape. But I knew that I had done it with the help of a friend. Somehow just being near him made me feel stronger, a man with a walking stick who seemed a symbol of a wisdom that had always escaped me.

We sat on a slab of rock, and Nelson opened his pack, pulling out a plastic container with two sandwiches wrapped in tinfoil. He handed me one. Famished from the steep climb, I opened it at once. It was a monster and still warm.

"Look at that," I said.

"That's your Reuben sandwich," Nelson said proudly as he began unwrapping his own. "It has your dark rye and Dijon mustard and sauerkraut. It has your corned beef and Swiss cheese. Buttered on both sides and grilled until the cheese melts. A side of sliced dill pickle."

I just nodded with my watery eyes. I knew that it was some kind of tribute, honouring me with a sandwich that bore my name, as if I had taken credit for its existence. I ate it with both hands, the juices running down my chin. You couldn't talk and eat a sandwich like that, such an orgasmic blend of sensations. The smacking lips, the chewing, and then the flood of taste, the absolute pleasure of good food on the tongue. Afterwards, we wiped our mouths and slick chins with napkins, while all around us ranged a visual feast. As we sat there I wondered about our friendship, for I felt content and wanted to be honest with Nelson.

I looked at him against the fissured rock, with its millennia of freeze and thaw. His rough skin was far beyond a youthful suppleness but still not yet ready to yield to the fragility that visits many his age, my age. He kept his body moving but idle long enough at the marina to chat a spell before answering some other impulse — a chore, a customer or a bright new day. I watched what he did, how he lived his life.

"Some time ago," I said at last, "when I was twenty-five, I ran down a young guy crossing the street. It was snowing really hard. I was in a hurry. It was my first day at a new job at Vancouver City Hall, and I didn't want to be late. I killed him. His name was Martin Rouse."

Nelson looked at me, no word from him right away, but I could see the changing expression on his face, the muscles around his eyes, inquiring, sorting out what he had just heard. "You killed him?" he said simply after a moment.

"Yes, with my father's truck."

"That's awful, Reuben."

"I don't know why I'm telling you this. I guess I just can't keep that from you anymore."

"I'm sorry that it happened."

"And the next year, Martin's brother Donny tried to kill my brother Lyle. He shot him in the leg with a rifle, crippled him for life. Donny spent seven years in prison for that. It turned out that he was crazy with grief and wanted to even things up."

"Damn," Nelson said. "All that?"

"Yes, all that. Do you remember my other brother, Walter, who came by the boat?"

"Nice fellow."

"Well, he looked after Lyle most of his life. Lyle had problems with alcohol. He was never the same. Walter had to put him in a home. That's a sad fact. And wouldn't you know it, Donny Rouse visited him, asked for his forgiveness. And Lyle gave it to him. Walter told me that Donny forgave me, too, for killing his brother. It's hard to make sense out of all that. It's something I have lived with, realizing the effect that day had on my family. And June stood by me the whole time. Never complained. I can't imagine forgiveness like that. I don't know where it comes from. It's just a word, but there must be a whole lot more to it. I'm wondering about Jonas. This whole story seems to come down to him. As if the universe is waiting for me to forgive him. I don't know, Nelson."

"This is what you call your deep water, Reuben."

"I didn't mean to dump it all in your lap."

"Don't worry," Nelson said solemnly.

I regretted that I had said too much. What was he to do with all that? I felt that I had just burdened a friend with the tragic story of my life, heaped it on him after that fine mountain dinner together. Soured it all. But Nelson was pondering, I could see, reaching for an answer for me.

"I can say that it saved me and Sal," he said after a time.

"How so?"

"It was a woman who hit us and killed Emily," he said. "I could have hated that woman all my life. And I was prepared to. That's the truth. We saw her when we were in court a few months after the accident. She had a sad story herself. Her husband was a logger and was decapitated by a choker up island. She had been drinking that day and Emily was just another tragedy for her. I was wild with bitterness and anger. But outside the courthouse I watched Sally push her wheelchair over to the woman and take her hand. I knew what she was doing. Right then and there I knew we had turned the page. 'We can understand anything with an open heart,' she said to me later."

"That's something," I said. The wind whooshed through the great firs around us.

"We're having dinner at the Greek place," Nelson said above the gusts. "You know, for my birthday. We'd like you to join us."

"My daughters will be in town. And their boyfriends."

"Bring them."

"Are you sure?"

"Not a problem. And no presents."

"Okay, no presents."

"Your new sails are in. I'll help you with them."

"Thanks."

"That's what you call your God there, Reuben." He swept the breadth of the sky with his hand.

I turned to him, something new.

We sat against the wall of rock, looking down on the backs of eagles and to a ship in the distance inching up the strait like a toy. Then it was gone. It seemed as though we were the last humans on Earth. Everything was ocean, trees and sky. And the sun slipping away.

The Book

THE TOWN WAS IMMACULATE in its summer glory, as if overnight
a team of Seaside devotees had scrubbed and cleaned the streets anew,
repainted the clapboard and trim, and made it a joy to be out along the
sidewalks on Main Street. A few days of rain did that. Then the sun
touched it all, the waterfront glistening, a lacquered world. There was a
rare happiness inside me, an optimism I seldom felt. The girls were
coming home. I was excited, readying the spare rooms and buying groceries, plenty of vegan things, just in case. Good God, I couldn't remember! June would have known, wrote me out a list. Did I ever pay attention, I wondered? I probably overdid it now, on my own, guessing. I
wanted to make their visit a special occasion, with wine, of course, beer
for the guys, and thick steaks that I hid in the freezer for the carnivores.
I had it all covered.

I walked down Main Street, looking in every store window, as if for
the first time. So many artisans contributed to the vibrant character of

Seaside. One could find the hands of creativity earnest in every back-room shop, home to eccentrics and the eclectics. They were like some estranged group of people, hippies perhaps, from my own generation, who had found sanctuary in simplicity, meaning in beautiful things. I was on my way to Salty Dog's Used Books. Muirgheal had something for me that I was anxious to see.

The bell rang inside the door. She was at the till as she always was, greeting you before your eyes could adjust to the dim light. No distracting breasts today.

"Well, I think you'll be pleased, Reuben," she said. "Not many like this anymore." She had it on the counter, a book in a plastic cover. She had her hand over it. "This is not any book, Reuben."

"No, it's not, Muirgheal. Well, let's see it."

"It was in San Diego, I think I told you before. It was located in the attic of an old house, in a bookcase with a sheet thrown over it. It was an estate sale. You buy these things unseen really. There's a brief description: you know, good condition and all that. Well, I have bought books in good condition with the spine coming apart and the corners dog-eared. But this is different." She kept her hand on the book, intent on telling its story.

Then she removed the plastic covering. "It came with its dust jacket," she went on, "the original book cover. As you can see, it's yellowed and torn. Someone added the plastic covering to protect it. But see what's inside."

She opened the book to remove the dust jacket. She set it aside and closed the book. It was mint, bold, black cloth board with silver stamped print — *Moby Dick* over a breaching sperm whale — all sharp definition and lustre. Black coated end papers, all edged in silver.

"And look at this," Muirgheal said. "It's the 1930 edition illustrated by Rockwell Kent." She opened the book once again to show me the illustrations — Ahab marching on his whalebone leg. Then she handed it to me.

I liked the feel of it, the weight, something over eighty years old in my hands. A nostalgic smell to it, breathing out from its plastic cover for the first time in years.

"It's in beautiful condition, Reuben," she said. "And look, Herman

Melville's name doesn't appear on the cover or the spine. Just there on the inside. And the woodcuts throughout, full page plates and . . ."

She was pleased with herself and I was delighted she had found it. "Thank you so much, Muirgheal," I told her. "It is beautiful."

She slipped the book into a cloth bag and placed it on the counter.

"Going green," she said. "I'll see if I can restore the dust jacket for you. A bit of that invisible tape."

"Thanks again." I took the bag and held the straps and looked down inside to see *Moby Dick*, a story there, but more, a man's idea from another time waiting the turn of a page. I turned to leave.

"So how did things turn out, Reuben?" Her voice lowered now.

"Are you the psychic or the bookseller?" I asked her.

"How about a friend?"

"You told me that night we can never know enough about another. I learned that much. But things did turn out . . . all that worry for nothing. And you said I was the strong one. That's not true. June was. That's something I always knew."

Muirgheal smiled, a knowing smile that bothered me, not because it wasn't pleasant or kind, but because she held back the words behind it.

When I returned home I went to the bookcase in the living room and pulled out the old *Moby Dick* paperback. I replaced it with the new book, the fat black spine of it dominating my aged collection on Dory Avenue, a prize to look at from across the room. Even Ishmael's narrative would seem better for it. I sat in my chair to admire it, how all the books looked in its company. Not many things satisfied me that way. Then I went and got it and returned to my chair.

I felt that I had been away, on a journey that had taken me far from home. This Seaside house no longer seemed so solid and familiar. It was not rich with memory, a place to hold you in the warmth of its enduring walls. Yet my things were all around me. They had filled a similar space in Kerrisdale, which still felt like home in a strange and appealing way. But I knew that I could never go back. How the mind makes the past better than it was. So where did I journey to and where was my home? I was home, I slowly began to recognize. I was making it *my* home, day by day.

I was sleepy, holding the book in my lap, feeling the weight of the story, remembering the voyage and the tragic ending. *From hell's heart...* The kids would arrive soon. They were on their way, somewhere out along the highway. Slow down on the curves, I was thinking. Be careful...

Family Matters

❧

I KNEW THE SOUNDS of the house, the fridge going through its range of cooling chatter, the clock in the kitchen shaped like an apple and its constant tic-tic, and the hot water tank with its gas-fired yawns. Common sounds in a hushed world, they evoked nothing. But the knock at the front door was no ordinary sound. And when I opened it, life rushed in like the breaching dam of my loneliness — and then Lori hugging me.

"How are you, Dad?" she was saying, bouncing and overjoyed.

"Fine, fine," I said wanting to look at her and seeing the smiling face behind her. He reached out with his hand.

"I'm Sean, Mr. Dale," he said solidly.

"Call me Reuben," I said taking his hand, his practised grip. I was looking up at him. "How was the trip up the coast?"

"It is so cool out here," he said.

"Of course I was the perfect tour guide," Lori said. They laughed at that, a private joke I was sure.

Then Mandy, so tentative, came up to me. "Hi, Dad," she said. A gentler hug.

I held her a little longer. I could feel her sadness. And there at her shoulder a reserved and anxious creature. She seemed reluctant to come forward.

"Dad," Mandy said, "this is Elise, my partner."

"Hello," I said.

A timid hand came out. "Pleased to meet you," she said with a lovely French accent.

I looked toward the rental car in the driveway and out into the street. There had to be someone else. But it seemed that everyone was account-ed for. Then I noticed Mandy holding Elise's hand, not fully, but by the fingertips. It confused me. She wasn't a business partner. Then it struck me. How could I have been so thick? I worried that Mandy could see the confusion in my face — what she had feared, what they both had feared.

"Come on in," I said, "come in." After they were all inside, I stood at the door for a moment before I closed it behind me. I looked out at the ordered street, the green lawns and beds of roses and listened to the rob-in carolling in Bert's cherry tree. A minute to reset myself and find the father that Mandy needed.

We assembled in the kitchen, of course, the town hall. Everyone seemed to be talking at once. There was so much to tell, so much catch-ing up to do. So I just listened. Oh, the energy of young people with their plans for the future, their dreams. Like her mother, Lori, animated and impassioned, began to coordinate the remainder of the day. She was happy, I could see. Sean seemed like a good young man, perhaps a little too eager to please her, I thought. But I suppose he had found out by now that it was easier that way. Mandy was more like myself, not so bold, and finding a place on the periphery. Then Lori led Sean out to the car for their suitcases and bags.

Mandy was watching me, her eyes asking something of me. Elise withdrew, not so inclined to dive dauntless into our family. It had to be now. But I couldn't find the right words for her, the right approach that would ease her awkward homecoming. So I moved to her and gathered the both of them into my arms, drew them close to me. I kissed their foreheads and looked into their eyes. We stood there and cried, huddled like that without a single word spoken, released our fears and trepidation, the anguish they carried, that I carried. We didn't notice Lori and Sean standing at the threshold of the kitchen with their teary grins.

Dinner was a sensation — not something I did, some culinary brilliance. It was the kids. Why do we call them that? They were young adults with a flair for improvisation, pulling things from the fridge, a bit of this and a bit of that. How they worked together, effortlessly, raising their wine glasses to toast yet another kitchen triumph. I so admired their sense of cooperation and their little acts of grace, inviting Elise to take her place in that shared blessing. It felt like a family again, an anchor for my drifting self-definition. I didn't want it to end. My life seemed to have been retrieved, made right, a correction in a flawed world. I was the centre of it all, a foundation from which they could build their lives. I was never that. But now it filled me with such purpose and wonder. I was drunk on prosperity. I wondered if June could see it all.

While Sean and Elise were cleaning up in the kitchen, Lori and Mandy drifted to my bedroom, the bedroom June and I had shared. They wanted to see. Absence is a powerful thing, a feeling of something no longer there, never to be there again. They stood at the door. They could feel it too, a trying moment to get beyond. I had laid June's clothes out on my bed. They were so cautious moving toward the outfits and sweaters, fingering the sleeves, stroking the fabric. The room seemed a museum, with clothes of the dead. It was supposed to comfort them, but it was sad and cruel somehow to know that the body of a person, a mother, a wife, had given fullness and life to the cottons and silks.

They stood a long time before they could pick up a blouse and bring it to their cheeks, to feel it, to smell her. I had done that very same thing and much more. I remembered the shame and mortification I felt, but I remained near them. They went through the jewellery. Lori chose a ring, her grandmother's cameo. June had worn it on special occasions. Mandy chose the angel pin she had given her mother one Mother's Day some time ago. They were not there to claim anything as their own. They both had a copy of the family portrait, and that was enough for them. Two small things, precious keepsakes. That's all they wanted.

"Dad," Lori said, "just put it all in bags and take it to a thrift store."

"Yes," Mandy said. "Someone could use them. They're still in perfect condition. Mom loved clothes."

"She was something when she was going out," I said. "Always dressed so, I don't know, sophisticated. You would notice her, the swing in her walk, the confidence. She was so capable. I wish I was like that."

Just then Lori and Mandy exchanged looks, some communication between them.

"Dad," Lori said, "you were like that but in a different way."

"Yes, Dad," Mandy said, "you were always there for us."

"Mom was always busy with school. She was never home."

"She tried to make up for it. We called her a lot on her cell phone. You know, girl stuff."

"Boys mostly."

"She had a demanding job," I said. I wasn't defending her so much as I was unable to recognize what they were saying.

"Yes, she did," Lori said, "and you did too, but you were often at home. We could always depend on you. You were there for us. Always."

"Whenever we were out," Mandy said, "we knew where you would be. Sitting down with a book. Just knowing that."

The hard remembering. It was a marvel to be in the presence of their maturity, young women. Lori looked the most like June, but she was her own person, nothing blurred there, and Mandy, well, she was following her heart. How perception varies. Were they talking about me? How could I live with them so far away?

"We're going up to the cemetery in the morning," Lori said.

"Place some flowers," Mandy said.

"I have to work down at the marina until noon," I said. "Then get the boat ready. There's new water to explore near Halfmoon Bay. The weather looks good."

"I can't wait to see *my June*," Lori said. "Sean's excited too. He's never sailed."

"Oh, and we have all been invited to a birthday dinner tomorrow night," I said.

"Who?" Lori wanted to know.

"The owner of the marina."

"Are you sure about that?" Mandy asked doubtfully.

"It's Nelson Grommet's seventy-fifth birthday. I think you'll like him."

"That's old," they both said.

Then Lori turned to me thoughtfully. "Did you ever take Mom's student sailing?"

The question caught me off guard. "Yes," I said. "It turned out fine."

We bagged the clothes and set them out in the garage. It felt as if we had removed that last part of her, moved her a little further away. Little steps of grief — one thing at a time. But it was still difficult to separate her from things. I thought that I would leave her clothes in the garage for the summer. Nothing final yet. I wondered if I would know when to take them away, discard what remained of her life. Then there would be a day when to find her would be to remember her. There is no solid reality in yesterday after all. The fruitless searching, all in vain. I was beginning to recognize that this understanding comes slowly. A lifetime perhaps.

Nelson's Birthday

∾

WE STOOD AT THE door putting on our shoes.

"So what's he like?" Mandy asked me.

"You'll see."

"What's his wife like?"

"You'll see."

"Are we too casual?"

"Don't think so. Nelson's not the one to get all dressed up for his birthday."

"Shouldn't we bring something?"

"I put it in your tote bag. Relax."

Mandy looked in the bag that was slung over her shoulder. "I can't relax," she said.

"I think that you got that from me. Sorry about that."

"I'm just a little nervous. You know, what they might think. What if he says something? Old people sometimes just come out with it. They're stuck in their outdated values. Oh, my God, listen to me, talk about stereotyping."

"It's all right," Elise said. "It'll be fine. We're fine."

"It's not a moral issue, Sis, you know that," Lori said.

"You're right."

On the way to the restaurant I started to think about what Mandy had said. *What if he says something?* Well, that was a damn thing to plant in my head. There I was, so mellow for once in my life, so at ease with the girls at home, with things going well in their lives. And now a chance to share a part of my life with them. Nelson wouldn't say anything, I was certain of it. But he had that innocent part of him, a quality that was not so predictable. I hadn't worried in a while, but it was coming back as we parked the car, my impressionable stomach doubting my good friend. And I felt bad for it: the complications that life brings, the dramas created in our silent imperfections. There was always something more that waited for its time.

A hostess met us inside the restaurant. I spoke to her briefly about the evening, Nelson's birthday. The room was full of diners abuzz with talking and laughter, but I couldn't find them until the hostess pointed to a couple sitting by a window overlooking the sea. Such a breathtaking contradiction, a delightful shock to see Nelson in a suit, and Sally exquisite in a purple gown. Her wheelchair was set aside. As we made our way across the dining room, Nelson stood to greet us. He looked so fine in his black suit with a tie to match Sally's dress. His often wind-blown hair was combed back, slick along his near-white temples. They seemed a couple from another era, the bearing of a count and baroness, how one might dine in the imagined world of a Hemingway novel.

"Reuben, thanks for coming," he said.

"Happy Birthday, Nelson," I said slapping him on the back.

"Thank you so much for joining us," Sally said, always her welcoming smile.

We sat down and I introduced everyone, so many names and new faces. That word *partner*. I nearly choked on it as hands reached across the table. Nelson standing for the girls. Then Elise's sweet voice. Nelson seemed to hesitate, some silent scrutiny, that possibility rising. Then words began to lift from his mouth. I stopped breathing. I watched, listened, but it was not a language I could fully understand.

"*Bienvenue à Seaside*," he said to her.

"*Vous êtes, les deux, si beaux ce soir.*"

"*Merci, et vous êtes belle, aussi.*"

Then Nelson took his seat and all seemed proper and good. The waitress came and set the menus down before us. I ordered wine for everyone. It was if the gods of emancipation had heard my nervous petition. It made me marvel at the man who sat across from me, his rusty but acceptable French.

"Don't mind us," Sally said. "We like to dress up for our birthdays. It's our time, you know, to feel kind of special. It might seem silly, but it's our night out on the town."

"You look so beautiful," Lori said.

"I really like the colour of your dress," Mandy said.

"A grand couple," Elise concluded.

"Why thank you," Sally said, "what charming young ladies."

Sally was overjoyed, something fulfilled in her sitting there, perhaps with thoughts of what could have been.

As we ate our dinners and we drank our wine, the talk flowed smoothly and warm. Sally had the ear of the girls with stories of how she met Nelson, back in the summer of 1964, in the Arctic when there was ice in the sea and adventure in their hearts. I could hear her small voice and her courage when she spoke about Emily. The girls softened even more to her, loved that tiny woman. I listened to Nelson and Sean. They shared their views on the state of our world, the tragic north and a government that had turned against the land for a false prosperity. I was an observer, a witness now, pleased just to watch it all.

When the waitress came by and took our plates, she looked at me, and I nodded, an arrangement I had made with the hostess. Then it came, sparkles and candles atop a chocolate birthday cake, and in the middle some white object that was not so recognizable, but a worthy attempt nevertheless. Nelson would know. When she set it down in front of him, a birthday chorus rose up and filled the dining room.

Nelson made a wish and blew out the candles. Looking carefully at that white chocolate figure in the middle of the cake, he just smiled. Then I motioned to Mandy, who reached into her bag and handed me Nelson's birthday present. I held it, felt it through the wrapping paper, and looked at him, saw something far off in his eyes. As if he knew.

"This is for you," I said.

His hand took it and still he looked at me, a humble man. "Didn't I say, no presents, Reuben?"

"It's not really a present, Nelson, it's a gift."

He nodded. He knew the difference. Then he turned to Sally and everyone leaned toward him.

"Open it, Nelson," Sally said. She rolled her eyes playfully.

He ripped the paper along its folds and pulled the paper free. And in his hands the book, the black brilliance of it, his fingers tracing the silver print of *Moby Dick*. He was dumbfounded, but his eyes were full of wonder. He touched the white whale on the cover with his fingertips. Then he opened it and stared down at what I had written. His bottom lip trembled, and he tried to stop it, but he could not. He read it out to us.

Happy Birthday, Nelson
I knew I would find you one day
Your friend Reuben

We were all drying our eyes as Nelson sat with his book. Sally patted his arm when she saw that the soft pouches under his eyes were wet. He held the book for a long time. It seemed that he was lost momentarily, in meaning and understanding, as if reconciling all the circumstances of his life since that day when Miss Peach brought him that book so long ago. He was the man who raised it with me in those early days down at the marina, told me quite earnestly how the ripples in one's life move in their unexplainable ways. But knowing that fact didn't make life much easier. Perhaps all it could do was to explain how things are intrinsically related in our world. Still, it was perplexing at times, I will admit, as I looked out the window to see Shirley Plath-Mellencamp walking along the promenade.

The setting sun was full on her tall body, with that raised chin and hair fanning over her shoulders and down her back. She seemed so sure that she knew where she was going. But I knew she struggled like the rest of us. I couldn't help regarding her. She intrigued me. I wouldn't say it was all a physical attraction. It was more a companionable thing to me, pilgrims along the way. And I wondered as I watched her, if loneliness could still exist if it were shared?

"Dad," Mandy said to me. She said it more than once to get my attention, noticed how I was craning my neck to watch her.

"Do you know her?" Lori asked.

They were all lifting from their chairs to look.

"Sort of," I said.

"Sort of?" Nelson said. "I don't think so, Reuben."

"I think he likes her," Mandy chimed.

"Are you kidding me?" I said. I couldn't admit such a thing in front of the girls. What would they think?

"Dad, what's wrong with that?" Lori said. "She looks attractive."

"Oh, she's that," Nelson said a bit too enthusiastically. He was no help.

"Nelson," Sally said swatting at his arm.

"Dad, it's okay," Mandy said.

I didn't say anything more. I didn't want them to see my flushed skin, my embarrassment. I thought that I would let it sink in, what they were saying to me. They were giving me permission, I knew. Bless you both, I thought to myself. I didn't know how they could move so easily around such complexities as loss and grief, and what comes next in a life. Perhaps my happiness was all that mattered to them. They were all smiles as Shirley disappeared from view. I don't think I had ever seen Nelson smile like that. It wasn't the Fourth of July fireworks on the beach. That was some other time and country. No, it was something very near.

Rapture of the Mariners

⚮

IT WAS A PERFECT DAY for sailing, blue skies and a good breeze. There was a stampede down the dock. Lori and Mandy couldn't wait to see her, running ahead, a spontaneous race between sisters. It was another homecoming for them. They hadn't been aboard *my June* since they had left for school. It didn't take them long to get reacquainted with her. They set out to explain the various ropes and rigging to Sean and Elise, a tour from bow to stern. I just watched them in a proud way. June was missing that most wanted thing in a life, I couldn't help thinking, to see children grown and magnificent, their full and breathtaking flight.

The girls were anxious to heave the lines and take *my June* out on the Salish Sea, flashing its rippling skin beyond the breakwater. Lori took her position at the wheel and started the motor. Mandy showed Sean and Elise how to pull the fenders, then untied the bow line and jumped aboard. I held the stern until *my June* came around. Looking about, I knew that I would see him somewhere among the boats, and there he was coming down the dock. I could see by his strides that he didn't want to miss our departure.

"Glad I caught you, Reuben," he said. "Here, I'll take the line and push you off."

"All right," I said. It didn't seem necessary to hurry down just to do that. I handed him the line and stepped over the stern rail. He was still holding the rope and looking at me funny like. "What is it?" I asked him.

"Nothing," he said. He tossed the rope to me and pushed us away from the berth. A little wave to the watching crew.

"Are you okay?"

"Thank you," he said.

"For what?"

"Thanks for what you did. Thanks for the book."

"You're welcome," I said, the space between us widening. "And thank you, Nelson."

"For what?"

I had to shout now. "For what you've done for me."

He turned and looked up and down the dock. I confused him per-haps. I don't suppose Nelson Grommet had set out to do anything in particular. That's what it was really, the fact that he trusted himself. He stood there watching us drift away. I looked up at the marina store, to the upper windows, and there, a tiny figure — Sally at her station. They were both watching us, perhaps not realizing the triangle that connected us just then. Were they imagining a day like that for themselves, their unobtainable dream? Perhaps they thought me the luckiest man in the world.

When we passed the breakwater I looked back to find Nelson gone. Then I turned to the sea, with Lori at the wheel. She silenced the little diesel when the mainsail was ready at the winch. Sean heaved, and up it came, the new sail, clean and bright. It caught the breeze, and there was life. All of us cheered. Then Mandy worked her way along the cabin to the headsail to free the sheets, while I assisted Elise and Sean at the halyard winch. I hadn't been on the water since the day Jonas flung his anger into the maw of the sea. Now with that memory of calamity and uncertainty, I was mindful of what a day could bring. The headsail unfurled from the forestay, and *my June* found her trim.

After we gathered along the stern rail, I watched them all with their continuous smiles. It was a thrilling time, I knew, to be out on such a day, under sail. I couldn't help looking at Lori, with her blond hair flagging in the wind, how it wrapped around her face at times, like her mother's when at sea. Then she would turn a certain way, and my heart would jump to my throat. The likeness was a trick it seemed, a fleeting moment when I believed that it was June standing there, and the world was made right again. And then I could feel Mandy, who knew what I was thinking, who had lived with that comparison all her life. I moved closer to her, slid along the rail and took her hand. Lori was watching us and smiled. Oh, the intimate life of sailors.

The breeze became a wind, and all was sea and mountains. "Make a course off the bay there, Lori," I said, "but keep her full in the wind."

"You need to take her, Dad," she shouted to me. "She wants to go."

I wasn't sure if the rising winds were too much for her, or if she just wanted to see me take the wheel, the patriarch. When I did so, she was pleased. It was not a title that came easily for me, neither an appointment nor an ordination. Still, I could feel an elder's mantle of responsibility. Perhaps even a wisdom that comes from having survived many of life's sorrows. Soon after, they all began looking ahead with the mountains growing before them. Halfmoon Bay opened like a gaping mouth, but we would not enter it on that day. *my June* was running fast. She heeled steeply all at once and Elise and Sean held onto the rail and howled the affirmations of baptized sailors. We sailed up the strait with alternating tacks carved into the sea like a skater's long and impossible strides. Porpoises appeared suddenly off the starboard beam, headlong and swift. They stayed there long enough for us to know their undulating rhythms and the awe of uncommon moments.

Lori and Mandy had been watching me, careful not to make it obvious. And when I made course for the very heart of the strait and the boom passed over me, I sensed they surely held their breath. I wondered if they thought about my mortality just then. It would be understandable, of course. Loss sharpens our sensitivities. But the sails popped, and

I raised a fearless chin to the wind the way a captain would to inspire confidence in his crew. A father does that for his children. I felt something certain in my life for the first time since that snowy morning on Cambie Street, the day I met their mother.

I turned and looked behind me, casually, to the wake trailing and receding, to my mistakes, familial omissions and suspicious miseries. I had to let them all go. It was time. I imagined Martin Rouse wouldn't mind so much. I had carried him for so long. Walter and Lyle, well, they deserved better from me. Life would go on as it will, events moving from one to the next, faithful and unstoppable. And my June, I would learn to live without her. But still I knew that she would always be with me, windward and eternal, running true into the immaculate blue days.

ABOUT THE AUTHOR

Danial Neil was born in New Westminster, British Columbia, in 1954 and grew up in North Delta. Already in his teens he began writing, and in 1987 he made the decision to become a full-time writer, taking his first Creative Writing course in Langley with Rhody Lake, and then studying Creative Writing at the University of British Columbia. Danial worked steadily at his craft, his first breakthrough coming when one of his short stories was published in the 2003 Federation of BC Writers anthology, edited by Susan Musgrave. He went on to participate in the Write Stretch Program with the Federation of BC Writers, teaching free verse poetry to children. He won the Poetry Prize at the Surrey International Writers' Conference four times. His first published novel was *The Killing Jars* in 2006. *Flight of the Dragonfly* followed in 2009, and *The Trees of Calan Gray* appeared in 2014. Both his fiction and poetry articulate a close relationship with the land, its felt presence a part of his narrative and vision. Danial lives in Oliver in the beautiful South Okanagan of British Columbia.

MARQUIS

Québec, Canada